Screen Idol

Hollywood to Olympus Book 1

Elle Rush

Copyright © 2014 Deidre Gould
All rights reserved under International and Pan-American Copyright Conventions.
Published in paperback by Deidre Gould
E-book published through Liquid Silver Books.
All rights reserved.
No part of this publication may be reproduced, stored in a retrieval system, or transmitted in any form or by any means, electronic, mechanical, recording or otherwise, without the prior written permission of the author.
This is a work of fiction. The characters, incidents and dialogues in this book are of the author's imagination and are not to be construed as real. Any resemblance to actual events or persons, living or dead, is completely coincidental.

ISBN: 978-0-9939904-0-3

.

Blurb

Sydney Richardson should have trusted her instincts and locked the door when a Greek god appeared on her doorstep at sunrise. After months of work, she needs every second of the day to wrap up a two-part fundraiser for burn victims like herself and she can't afford to waste time with a TV hunk, no matter how good he looks in a toga.

Chris Peck, worshipped by millions as Zeus on the hit drama Olympus, desperately wants to prove to the producers of a soon-to-be-cast romantic comedy that he doesn't need fight scenes or special effects to make the jump to the big screen. Acting as the slave-for-a-day in the show's fan appreciation contest was supposed to cement his everyman credibility but the winner wants nothing to do with him.

Chris is captivated the woman who refuses to fawn over his looks and fame, and he promises to put her fundraising efforts over the top if she'll spend the day with him. However, just when he convinces Sydney they could have a chance together, the movie's producers offer him an audition that would mean breaking his promise and leaving Sydney in the lurch. The king of the gods has until sunset to prove to his new off-screen love interest that Hollywood magic and reality can co-exist.

Dedication

To Barb, who was the first to read Chris and Sydney's story, and then helped make it better.

Chapter 1

There shouldn't be a six in the morning on a Saturday unless you stayed up for it after an exhausting, exhilarating Friday night. It was a rule somewhere. If a person were demented enough to get up before daybreak on a weekend, there were only three acceptable reasons: a newborn, a paycheck, or a fire alarm. Answering the door didn't make the list. Nobody should ever knock on someone else's door at such a perverse hour. It was uncivilized, but since the moron in question seemed to be unaware of this polite societal convention, it was up to Sydney Richardson to educate him. Possibly with a brick to the cranium.

She had planned this Saturday down to the minute, and she needed every second of it. Her precise schedule was supposed to start with her alarm going off at six fifty-two, allowing her a single eight-minute snooze cycle before she rolled out of bed at seven on the dot to hit the shower. This was the first weekend in a month that she hadn't pulled an extra shift or two, and neither Saturday's nor Sunday's to-do list had "answer the door before sunrise" on it.

This was the weekend. Months of blood and sweat and tears and migraines had gone into today's events. She'd started her charity with the hope of raising enough money to help one or two people afford the same medical procedures that got her out of the hospital and back to her life. The snowball effect had caught her unaware. The more she raised, the more people got involved and the bigger things got, until the small fundraiser had become a multi-part, day-long fundraiser with dozens of volunteers who all looked up to her. She wasn't going to let anyone down today—not her donors, not her volunteers, and absolutely not the people she was supposed to be helping.

But it wasn't supposed to start yet.

Sure, now she was awake a whole hour early, but she'd stayed up half an hour later than she intended to the night before and watched an old M*A*S*H re-run after she'd come home from a girlfriend's birthday party at Yellow Fin Sushi. Sydney had told her body it could sleep until seven, and now it got back at her for lying by walking her into the open closet door. Dammit. After grabbing her robe and feeling her way out of the bedroom, she ricocheted off the wall between the framed Beverly Hills Cop and Raiders of the Lost Ark posters on the way down the hall. At this rate she might not make it to the door.

Her cupcake nightshirt didn't matter, she thought as she limped through the house. Her red hair pulled into a Pebbles Flintstone-style ponytail on the top of her head didn't matter. The plastic framed glasses she had to jam on to find her way down the main hall since she wasn't stopping to put in her contacts didn't matter. What mattered was making the pounding on her door go away so she only had to deal with the Japanese drumming group inside her skull. Sake was evil.

She peeked through the peephole and spied a man in a black tuxedo. A suit she would have ignored, but the shock of a tuxedo woke her up a little. She squinted and took a second look: tall, dark hair, light eyes. He was very handsome in a movie star kind of way. At least, Sydney assumed he was handsome. The fish-eyed view and lack of caffeine might have been coloring her perception. "Who are you?"

"Your slave for the day."

It was much too early for this. "What the hell are you talking about?"

"I'm Chris Peck."

"You look like him. Kinda. Why are you at my house?"

"I'm really Chris Peck. I play Zeus on Olympus. You entered the show's sweepstakes on the network website and won first prize of a Greek slave for the day, namely yours truly. You got a confirmation call to expect your slave from sunrise to sunset today."

Her synapses started to fire. Slowly. Olympus was a hit primetime cable drama about a group of Greek gods on Mount Olympus during the decline of Greece's golden age. It was part Spartacus, part Game of Thrones, and part Hercules. She had submitted a ton of entries to the sweepstakes. They were offering a $1000 DVD library of historically-based television shows and documentaries as second prize. The first place prize never even registered because she wasn't a diehard fan of the show.

She watched it semi-regularly. She liked a lot of the actors but despised one in particular, so it came out a wash. To be honest, the only ones she made sure not to miss were the episodes where her favorite drama actor was guest starring as Dionysus. Seeing the defunct FBI show's once team leader playing the god of sex, drugs, and rock 'n' roll in a toga was a beautiful thing to behold. Sydney enjoyed splashing around in the shallow end of the pool on occasion, and she wasn't ashamed to admit it.

She hadn't paid much attention to the show's lead actor. In hindsight, that might have been a mistake, because the king of the gods was standing on the other side of her front door, and—from what she could tell—he was heavenly.

Sydney flipped the deadbolt off and cracked open the door, leaving the security chain on. She rubbed her bleary eyes and repositioned her glasses. It was definitely him.

Chris Peck. Zeus. The peephole didn't do this guy any favors. He was much cuter in person than he looked on television. Taller too. And not in a toga. Whoever had said that a well-tailored suit was to a woman what lingerie was to a man hadn't been kidding. His tuxedo was giving her some naughty ideas about going back to bed that had nothing to do with an extra hour of shut-eye. It had been a very long while, but she was pretty sure when a clean-cut, brown-haired, hazel-eyed Greek god magically appeared on a woman's doorstep, sleep was not the first thought that should come to mind. It wasn't. Unfortunately, tingles or no tingles, she had too much on her to-do list to waste any time on a toga party fantasy, let alone on an actual god at the door. Sydney tilted her head and stared at him. "Wow. You really are Chris Peck."

She was rewarded with a blinding smile. "And you are Sydney Richardson. At least I hope you are, because if you aren't this is really embarrassing."

"What do you mean I got a call? Nobody called me," she insisted. If she'd won a prize, they should have at least contacted her to make sure she'd be home for delivery. This was a hell of a delivery.

"Yes, they did. My assistant says she did. She left a message confirming the date and time. And she sent flowers."

"No, she didn't."

"Yes, she did."

Tuxedo Boy was going to argue with her before she'd had any coffee? "I'm pretty sure I would have remembered somebody telling me I was going to have a slave show up at the butt crack of dawn on a Saturday," she snapped. There was no way in hell she would have agreed to this Saturday. Next weekend, or the one after that, would have been much more convenient. Today was absolutely not an option.

The suicidal actor opened his mouth to defend himself again when Sydney waved him off. "Wait a minute." It was difficult to push through the fog without any caffeine, but there was something there. "Is your assistant's name Kristin?"

"Yes."

"There was a message on my machine, on Wednesday, I think. Some girl named Kristin said she was cancelling my regular nine o'clock appointment on Saturday. She didn't leave a number. Since I don't know a Kristin, and I didn't have any regular appointments scheduled, I didn't worry about it. I think the message is still on my voicemail." Sydney smiled in victory. She had a memory like a steel trap. A rusted trap, on occasion, but it was working fine this morning.

"Oh, crap."

"What?"

"It sounds like my fight trainer got a dozen roses and a note saying I was looking forward to my day of servitude."

She wasn't pleased to be awake, and this whole waste of time was a pain in the ass, but that was pretty funny. "Maybe she likes roses."

"His name is Russ, and he's former navy. I'm thinking not. So how can I serve you this morning?"

Sydney stood corrected. This was hilarious. It was always good to begin the day with a laugh. It set the tone for what followed. Now that she was up she had the chance to get a jump start on her list. With some juggling, she could shift her first appointment of the day forward, which would gain her about half an hour. Her schedule had been tight to the point where a couple minutes could have cost a bus connection and thrown off her entire afternoon. This could work in her favor. All she had to do now was send Zeus on his way.

Sydney stifled a yawn. "You could leave. I'm sorry about the missed message confusion, but today isn't going to work for me. Maybe you could have your assistant contact me again and we could reschedule. Happy Valentine's Day."

She shut the door in his face. If this was a regular hangover hallucination, she'd have to drink sake more often.

*

This was what his life coach would call a learning experience, Chris Peck thought. Not that he needed a life coach, but his agent had hired one to try to curb Chris' impulsive tendencies when it came to, well, everything. His coach's most recent attempt was to get Chris to take a "you get what you give" karmic approach to life. So far this morning, Chris was beginning to understand that despite his publicist's repeated affirmations, there was a girl on the planet who would give him the cold shoulder and treat him like the mere mortal he was, and not the god he pretended to be.

Perhaps he shouldn't have expected her to fall at his feet at six in the morning just because he was Chris Peck.

Although it had always worked in the past. He never had trouble with women. His publicist called him irresistible, and she was right. Chris was known for his looks—his face and his abs were his best features. All the magazines said so. He'd even made the "top ten sexiest men on television" issue this year.

Maybe Miss Richardson was wearing the wrong glasses.

No, that wasn't a karmic thought. Chris had done

something to earn this. Having the door shut in his face could be payback to teach him humility for the hubris his life coach kept warning him about. Maybe it was arrogance that led him to bet his fellow gods and goddesses that he ruled at both Olympus and karaoke. Perhaps if he'd kept karma in mind before he took the microphone, he wouldn't have humiliated himself and been voted unanimously as the worst singer in the cast, and he would have ended up as one of the hosts for the show's charity golf tournament instead of being the sweepstakes prize. Because this was truly humiliating. He was a leading man begging for some stranger's attention as if he were back at his first audition.

That must be it.

He couldn't blow the woman off either, not after all the effort and campaigning he and his agent had done for him to even be considered by High Note Productions for their new romantic comedy. The tabloids were already predicting the leading role going to one of two big name actors, despite the fact neither had shown any public interest in the part. Chris wasn't even under serious consideration as far as the press was concerned. He knew he had the range as an actor to be seen as more than a competent episodic action player. What he needed was a very public showcase for his rom-com talents. He needed the producers to see him sweeping a complete stranger off her feet in real life to prove he could do it on film. Playing "slave" was his shot. But he couldn't prove anything to anyone if Miss Richardson wouldn't play along.

No, he corrected himself. She wasn't responsible for his problem. She held the solution in her hands, but he had to earn it by finding the karmic way.

He ran his finger under the collar of the tuxedo shirt.

He'd put a tux back on at five in the morning in the past while making a getaway after a one-night stand, but he'd never purposely dressed in one at this hour. He brushed off a couple stray brown hairs from his haircut the night before. He had to be "pretty" for today, his publicist had told him. Pretty. He really hated that word.

Chris shot a quick look to the photographer/social network intern standing off to the side. The sweepstakes winner hadn't even noticed the short Hispanic teenager with the shaved head and camera bag on the sidewalk when she answered the door. "Let's try a second take."

The studio trainee, Benny Duarte, shrugged at him and raised his camera. "Works for me. She shut you down so fast I missed it."

Punk. Chris knocked again.

The response was quicker this time. "Yes?" she said through the crack.

"We can't reschedule."

"Then I guess I'll have to forfeit the prize. Sorry you wasted the trip."

She was closing the door again. "Wait!" What was wrong with this woman? If she'd been paying attention, or had been more awake, she wouldn't have missed the desperation in his voice. Couldn't she cut him some slack? It wasn't his fault his assistant had messed up. He had to convince her to cooperate. "There are a lot of Olympus fans who would die for this opportunity." Didn't everyone hope that celebrity rubbed off? This was La-La Land; Chris thought a desire for fame was a mandatory for residents.

"Great. Call one of them and ask if they are willing to be a last minute replacement."

Guess not. "I would but we already put your name in the press releases. Look, the PR department even sent a photographer to document the mortal getting the Greek god as a slave for a day." Chris pulled the teenager into her line of vision. "Benny Duarte, this is our sweepstakes winner, Miss Sydney Richardson."

"Hi," the intern sputtered.

"Hi. Still not interested."

Then she yawned at him. Again. Sure, she covered her mouth and excused herself but really?

"You're going to be in magazines as a woman who bossed around Zeus. Maybe even be on television," Chris bribed.

"I don't have time to be on television. I'm busy."

"Sydney—may I call you Sydney? I know the arrangements got messed up, but we can't cancel the publicity arrangements. It wouldn't be fair."

"Not fair to whom? Life's not fair. Shit happens," Sydney countered.

"Wear a hat," Chris finished.

"Exactly." She looked rather impressed that he knew the expression. Then she opened the door a little wider.

He'd take that as a good sign. "You said you don't have time for this today. I'm literally here to offer you a hand. Two of them." He held out both hands. "Maybe we can help each other out. Seriously, as long as it's not illegal, I'll do it if you let Benny take some photos. A couple of jobs and I'll be out of your hair, I promise." Technically, he was supposed to hang around until sunset, but a couple of hours should be enough to convince the High Note people. Chris couldn't believe he was pleading for the chance to do scut work. The things he did for a role. *Please, miss, let me take out your trash or wash your car…*

"I have a bus pass. I don't have time to go buy enough tickets to shuttle you around the city all day."

"I have a car."

That stopped her in mid-excuse. Her eyes opened wider at his vehicular pronouncement. He started to think he had her. Then a look so mercenary crossed her face that he took a step back. Maybe he didn't want her after all. She was scarier than Layla Andrews, his television wife, when she was having a bad hair day, and there was little scarier than that pint-sized Filipino actress on a bad hair day. Sydney wasn't having a great hair day herself by the looks of it, but her tousled bed head look was definitely doing it for him.

She held up a finger and closed the door enough to remove the chain. When she opened it fully, he saw a hallway lined with movie art of eighties blockbusters, and an old-school, glassed-in fire extinguisher box mounted on the wall.

"You have access to a car? And we can use it to run my errands this morning? I have five hours of non-stop running around to do before my day gets really busy, and I have to be done by noon. Do you have a license?"

"I have a driver. 'I've got a full tank of gas and half a pack of cigarettes. The sun's up so we can wear sunglasses'." If the Blues Brothers poster inside was a sign of a legitimate fan, she'd recognize the altered quote.

"I'm home by twelve?" Sydney repeated.

"I promise."

She nodded at him and then finished the movie quote. "'Okay. Let's hit it'."

Then she shut the door in his face again. But only for a moment this time. She reopened it and thrust a handful of bills at him. "Your first job today is to go to Bella Bean on the corner. I think they open at six on Saturdays so you should be fine. Get me a super grande cinnamon latte, please. Say yes to the first choice of every option they give you. And a sugar-crusted cranberry scone. Don't forget to get something for yourself." She pointed at Benny. "Get something for him too. We're going to be running today. Take twenty minutes, okay? I can be ready by then."

"Okay," Chris agreed quickly. He couldn't afford for her to change her mind.

She shut the door.

"This is going to be a very long day," he said to Benny.

Chapter 2

It was a nice little neighborhood. There was an equal split of smaller chain places and independent restaurants and stores. The houses and apartment blocks were older but well maintained. He and Benny made it to the sidewalk before they realized the woman hadn't told them which corner.

"Left or right?" Benny asked.

"It doesn't matter. We have time for both."

Chris veered left. The coffee shop was at the far end of the street. Benny hung back as he stepped up to the cash register to get a few pictures of him placing the order. "A grande cinnamon latte, please," he said to the tattooed barista with the "Marco" nametag.

"Skim milk or whole milk foam?"

"Skim."

"Caramel or chocolate sauce?"

"Caramel."

"Double cupped or cardboard sleeve?"

"Double cupped. And a sugar-crusted cranberry scone too, please."

"So, you know Sydney?"

"Yes." Wait. What? "How did you come up with that?"

"Syd is the only customer at this hour who gets the skim milk foam and the caramel sauce with a cinnamon latte. The scone just sealed the deal. But she doesn't come in on the weekends," tattooed Marco said.

"I'm picking it up for her," Chris explained.

"In a tux?"

The barista with purple hair at the espresso machine looked him over. "Oh my God, you're Chris Peck. Everybody, it's Chris Peck!"

"I am."

"Holy shit, are you dating Sydney?"

Chris wasn't surprised that the redhead had made an impression on the barista. He'd only met her for a few minutes, and even with no makeup and her hair not done, he could see how unforgettable she was. The short baby-blue silk robe over her thigh-high nightshirt hadn't hurt either. "No, we're not dating. She won the Olympus sweepstakes, and first prize was a mortal fan getting a Greek god to act as a slave for a day. She sent me on a coffee run."

Tattooed Marco nodded as if it made sense. "She's been talking about that contest for a couple weeks. She really wanted to win—"

"Dammit!" the purple-haired barista yelled. She threw the cup she was holding into the sink beside her and turned on the cold water tap full force.

"Are you okay?" Benny asked her, coming up to the counter.

She turned, and Chris spotted her nametag. It said "Barney".

"I'm good. The steamer spits like a bitch sometimes." She brushed her bangs out of her eyes and gave the photographer a coquettish smile.

Seriously? She was flirting with a barely shaving intern while a bona fide Greek god in a tuxedo was standing right in front of her? It was official. This was the worst day of his career. And that included the "Nair for Men" commercial he got as his first gig.

While Benny gave purple Barney his order, tattooed Marco informed Chris that he was also an actor. While he waited for his change, Chris was treated to what he thought was supposed to be a Robert DeNiro impression, from "Meet the Parents" if he wasn't mistaken. After that, Chris grinned and bore it while several customers took pictures on their cell phones of him playing personal assistant. He was lucky; fetching coffee ranked pretty low on the possible embarrassment scale. He stuck around for a handful of autographs before giving his regrets about having to get back to his duties. He wondered how long it would be before one of the various press outlets picked up the photos from Twitter or Facebook. He hoped that Benny's uploads to the show's sites were first. It would drive traffic and make him look better.

Karma, man, he said to himself. Humility. He could tell he'd be learning lots of humility today. He'd be happy to learn it if it landed him the High Note lead. If he did this good deed and followed through on this crap job now, he would be repaid. Doing a latte run in a tuxedo could be considered romantic, if people looked at it right. And squinted hard. "I can't believe I'm going to be doing shit like this all day," Chris grumbled to the intern. He could learn and gripe at the same time. There was nothing unkarmic about that.

"It could be worse. Technically, according to the terms of service of the sweepstakes, she could ask you to wear your costume all day. I saw a pool when we pulled up to her complex. Imagine yourself in a toga waving a palm frond over her in between serving her frothy drinks on a silver tray."

Chris stopped dead in the middle of the sidewalk. "If even a hint of that crosses your lips, you'll be doing promo work for Roadkill Kitchen until you hit puberty."

Benny gulped. "I won't say a word."

The sun was coming up on the return trip. Chris was surprised at the amount of foot traffic considering the hour. They'd dodged a cyclist, a jogger with a retriever on a leash, and a double baby stroller by the time they got back to her unit. As they backtracked, he noticed the row houses on Sydney's street all had bright flowers in window boxes. Hers were red and yellow. They were nice. The houses looked much more lived-in than the sterile apartments in Burbank where he rented.

Too soon, Chris plastered on another smile and held the tray of coffees up like a pro. "Let's see what our winner is like when she's awake."

He was getting tired of knocking on this door.

* * * *

That had to be one of the fastest showers in history. Thank God she'd shaved her legs the night before since she knew she was going to be on the beach playing volleyball all afternoon. Now Sydney was stuck in front of her closet in a jam. What did one wear for spending the day in the company of a television star who would be playing the role of one's personal servant? The guy could make her look bad if he was wearing a sack, forget about competing with a tuxedo. Jeans were too frumpy, and she wanted to look good. Well, as good as Jane Average could look standing next to a Greek god.

Her hand moved to the next hanger with no conscious thought. A nice dress would be ideal but utterly impractical for the errands she had to get done today. She swished past blouses and skirts and slacks. Her wardrobe had shrunk significantly in the last year as she'd started to cover more skin when she went out, but Sydney hadn't realized now she'd sacrificed sexy along with revealing. She was paying for that oversight now. She hesitated when she hit a green, brown, and white capris and cotton knit combo.

That would work.

She was in the bathroom when the knocking on her front door started again. "Be right there!" she shouted.

She still took a moment to double-check herself in the mirror. Her glasses were gone, and her contacts were in. She'd gotten rid of the Pebbles ponytail, and her strawberry blonde hair was plaited into a French braid that was tucked under and pinned at the base of her neck. She'd put on eyeliner and mascara to make her hazel eyes pop a little for the camera, and then enough blush and lipstick to give herself some color. Foundation was great at night, but during the day it wasn't worth it to try to tone down her freckles.

She leaned in to the mirror and checked again. It used to be she'd glance and go, but her self-confidence had vanished with her old clothes. Every day she fought to get a piece of her old life back. She'd already planned to force herself out of her comfort zone today. Karma seemed to be rewarding her determination by throwing this contest her way to make sure she didn't back out of her decision.

Sydney looked at the clock on the microwave. It said 6:38 a.m. If she was going to be up this early, she was going to make the most of it. She grabbed her purse, keys, and white straw hat off the kitchen table, hook in the entryway, and closet shelf respectively. It was time to get down to business.

She opened the door to find the actor holding the coffee tray out toward her. He presented the bag of pastries with a flourish. "Miss Richardson."

"Thank you, Mr. Peck. Shall we sit outside and have breakfast?" Wow, she was overdoing the formal stuff. Sydney was prepared to admit she was more than a little star-struck at the thought of buying coffee for a movie star. Really, who plans for that on a random Saturday? She stepped out to greet him.

The photographer kid reached for her door. It was

most likely a polite gesture since her hands would be full once she accepted the coffee tray, but she hip-checked him before he touched the knob. "We won't be eating inside. And we definitely won't be taking any photos of the inside of my house."

"I only need a couple shots," Benny protested.

"I didn't have time to put away everything that has identifying information on it. I don't need a partial credit card statement or my home address appearing in the background of a publicity photo. Outside is okay, so long as you don't publish the street or neighborhood."

"Benny, no. The outside of your home will be fine, Sydney," Chris interrupted.

Sydney offered him her first real smile of the morning. "Thank you, Mr. Peck."

"Just Chris."

"Sure, Chris." See, she could do this. It's not like he was a drop-dead gorgeous movie star with millions of fans or anything. Absolutely he could be Just Chris if he wanted to. But now that they'd introduced themselves, what else did they have to say to each other?

The front steps faced east so they were treated to a stunning, smog-less view of the sun breaching the farthest skyscrapers. Sydney peeled the lid off her cinnamon latte and let the first waft of steam hit her nose. She hoped to be inspired by the caffeine. "Cinnamon, skim milk foam, caramel sauce, double-cupped. Perfect." She set it on the step beside her without taking a sip.

She opened the paper bag with the Bella Bean logo on either side and found three smaller matching bags. The first was a sugar-crusted cranberry scone. She shrugged off Chris' amused look and didn't hesitate to break off a corner and pop it into her mouth. Paychecks and pastries were the only things worth getting up for. She set the little bag against her coffee cup and fished another out. She peeked into it and held it up to be claimed. "Which one of you made a new friend this morning?" Sydney turned the bag so they could both see the "Barney—310-555-8908" scrawled in black marker.

Benny sheepishly held out his hand. "What? She was cute."

"She had purple hair," Chris said.

Sydney looked at the last items in the bag. "I think they forgot your order, Chris. There's only a yogurt and a spoon in here." She noticed Benny had backed off a couple steps, but she was more concerned about starving her slave for a day.

"That's all I wanted."

"No muffin? No bagel? No scone? Did I short you on the cash?" God, please let her not have made him pay for his own breakfast.

"Wheat-free diet," Chris explained. He sat up a little straighter and rolled his shoulders as he reached for his yogurt.

"Wheat-free diet? No wheat? No flour? No cake?" Sydney exclaimed. No cake! That was horrible. And appalling. It was unfathomable in all honesty. "What the hell kind of life is that?" She tossed him the big bag, then picked up the little one containing her scone and clutched it to her chest. She broke off another piece and savored it slowly. "That's a terrible diet. Besides, you don't need it."

"Thanks."

It was true. Between the shirt and the jacket, she couldn't see a six-pack, but the guy spent all day in front of a camera wearing a toga. He probably had the arms to match. He definitely had a tan that a white toga would set off. It was a real tan too, not a booth-generated or sprayed-on one. Chris was old-school movie star good looking: tall, dark, and handsome. If it were just based on appearance, it would be no hardship to spend the day staring at him. But if they were going to be interacting, she hoped there was more. Looks weren't everything. She knew that.

"If you want to follow somebody's nutritional advice, try Oscar Wilde," she suggested. What was with her today? Open mouth, insert foot.

"And what does a dead playwright have to say about nutrition?" Chris asked with a smile.

"Everything in moderation, including moderation," Sydney said. "It works for me." She took a big bite of the scone and got a mouthful of cranberries. Damn, that was tart, even with the sugar crust.

Chris gave her a funny look, and she realized she'd scrunched up her face in reaction to the blast of sourness. She swallowed a couple times, choking on the dry pastry. Then she took a smaller, cranberry-free bite.

The Wilde diet did work for her. Nobody was going to mistake her for an actress. She didn't have the one percent body fat thing going on. She had muscles and curves and all her original parts, not including a capped tooth and some fillings. She was more than pleased to slide from a size eight into a size six on occasion, if the cut of the dress was right, but she wasn't going to kill herself by sacrificing flour to do it. If she were to get in front of a camera she'd have to lose fifteen pounds, but right now in the real world, she felt she was a pretty damned good size and shape.

She heard a series of faint clicks and looked down the walkway. Now she understood why Benny had backed off. While she was flipping out about the thought of a cakeless life, he'd been taking candid shots of her and Chris on the steps. The actor's shoulder twist had been to improve the shot. She hadn't even realized what was going on. That must be the difference between her and someone who spent his life in front of a camera. She wondered if Chris had even realized what he'd done.

"What do you do for a living, Sydney?" he asked.

"I work in a call center. It's very unglamorous." She jumped to her feet and brushed a couple stray crumbs off her lips. She couldn't match the excitement of his job. Well, she assumed it would be exciting when he wasn't being offered up as a sweepstakes prize.

Speaking of, she'd promised to let Benny take pictures of them doing things in exchange for Chris lending her his chauffer and limo. She should get started. "Are you a cat person or a dog person?"

Chris climbed to his own feet. "Cat?"

"Great, because snack time's over and we have to get to work. But first we have to get you out of those clothes." Sydney tipped the cup back and drained the last of her latte.

Chapter 3

"That's not part of the services offered." There it was. Chris had been expecting a freaking-out OMG-you're-famous reaction, especially since he'd arrived unannounced. He had that effect on fans, but Sydney had been treating him like a real person, which was a nice surprise. He would have bet cash money that the whole cake interlude had been legitimate. He'd already made a note not to get between this woman and any desserts. But, no, he wasn't a human being after all—not to her. His smile vanished.

He was scowling so hard it took a moment for him to realize that she was flapping her hands up and down as she tried not to spew a mouthful of coffee.

"No! No, no, no, not what I meant!" she sputtered. "I don't want to see you naked. Not that you wouldn't look good naked. I'm sure you look really, really good naked. God, I probably can't say that, either. What I meant was that you can't wear a tuxedo—not where we're going. Do you have any normal people clothes?"

Now he was almost offended that the cute redhead didn't want to see him out of his tuxedo. He'd never had any complaints before. Or anyone turn him down at all. He checked out what she was wearing. The nightwear had been endearing, but this outfit had the "classy casual and I'm not trying that hard" vibe. She wore it well. The green and brown set off her eyes. When she smiled, they got cute little crinkles at the corners. Her braid wasn't as sexy as the ponytail had been, though. "Sure. I brought something to wear after I was done here."

"Unless they're club clothes, they'll probably be a lot better for running around in."

Christ, he was confused. She wanted him to look like

a regular person when they were out in public together? Chris couldn't think of the last time that had happened on a date. Maybe before his Rebel Wing days, while he was still scrambling for guest spots. All of his girlfriends since then seemed to want to go out with him for the press coverage.

Not that Sydney was a girlfriend. This was a photo opportunity. Chris considered the change of clothes he'd packed. He supposed they would do for an everyday look, but he'd hoped to make a better impression in the photos. The penguin suit was a pain in the ass, but it would show he had a sense of humor about the "slave for a day" event, and that was what he was going for. Looking average was average. He'd have to compensate for the comfort.

His train of thought derailed when Sydney laid her hand on his sleeve. Judging by the concern on her face, he must have been wearing a highly insulted look.

"It's not that you don't look all Double-Oh-My-God in that tux," she offered as a compliment. "But it's totally going to get ruined, and while I can spring for coffee I can't afford a replacement Hugo Boss." She patted his arm. "Is that okay?"

The whiplash this woman was putting him through was going to cause permanent damage. He hadn't expected flattery, and the last time someone was genuinely concerned about him was probably when he was living at home. He patted her hand back. "So what exactly are we going to be doing that will ruin a tuxedo?"

"Well, you did say you liked cats."

"Are you going to explain about the cats?"

"Maybe we should discuss the sweepstakes' rules and terms of services before I step on another landmine. I read them at the time but…"

He cut her off. "You actually read those things?"

"You don't?"

Okay, that wasn't him being impulsive. Nobody read those things. "Not really."

"You should. Microsoft probably owns your first born at this point. But I digress. The rules seemed pretty basic. No sex, no nudity, no sexual contact, no sexual harassment."

Today was sounding like less and less fun. "Who determines sexual harassment?" Chris asked.

"I'd assume the person on the receiving end."

"For the record, I'll accept hugs. Maybe a kiss with no tongue at the end of the day if you ask nicely."

Sydney cocked her head and raised an eyebrow. "What makes you think I'll be doing the asking?"

* * * *

Chris pulled off his bowtie. Now he was thinking about kissing Sydney. Kissing her and cats. Not kissing cats, just cats in general. He didn't hate felines. He didn't have an opinion about them at all. He'd never owned one as a pet. He unbuttoned his shirt and slipped it under the jacket that was already on the hanger swinging from the shower curtain rod. He pulled a black golf shirt out of his gym bag and shook the wrinkles out of it before he put it on. It worked with his khakis. It wouldn't make any best dressed lists, but he'd look good in Benny's photos.

He checked himself in the bathroom mirror. His new haircut was so short that pulling a shirt over his head couldn't mess it up. He was reaching for the doorknob when one of his worst habits got the better of him.

The medicine cabinet screamed for a peek.

It was an invasion of privacy. He knew it was. And he valued his enough to know it was wrong. But it was like fudging your taxes. Everybody did it, but nobody talked about it. There was the private you never told anyone, and there was the private you knew was out there that people could find but you hoped they would never mention in public.

Sydney's cabinet had a magnetic clasp.

His had a miniature digital lock. Of course, he knew what he was hiding, and ninety-nine percent of the people who entered his house would mention what they found in public or, more likely, sell the information for a hefty price tag if they had photos as proof.

All this would do was give him some insight into the woman he was obliged to spend the day with. Technically, he was making sure the event went as smoothly and successfully as possible. He was doing them both a favor.

Chris opened the door.

The bottom shelf was disappointingly normal. Spare lady razors, headache and cold medicine, half a sheet of blister-packed allergy tablets, and a nearly empty box of bandages. The second shelf was a bit more interesting with large bottles of mega doses of vitamins C, E, and B complex. There was an old bottle of antibiotic as well. The rest of that shelf and the one above it were crammed with creams. Glass jars and plastic tubes full of aloe, gotu kola, calendula, vitamin K, and a dozen brands he'd never heard of. He'd seen makeup artists with less variety. He didn't even know what gotu kola was. But it was probably on the jar.

He was fumbling with the glass container when the phone in his pants pocket rang. He jammed the gotu kola back into the cabinet and slammed the door shut. "Chris Peck," he greeted when he recognized the caller ID as the studio's public relations department.

He "yupped" and "okayed" and generally faked his

way out of the bathroom, through the main floor to the front door. Someone, some nameless person that he was going to track down and shoot later, had convinced Martine Peeples of the PR department that having a photographer assigned to the "slave for a day" sweepstakes winner was not enough. Now they wanted him and Sydney to come to the set for a presentation and photo shoot. He had barely convinced her to let him hang around for just the morning. How was he supposed to talk her into giving up two hours of her afternoon to do him an even bigger favor when the whole prize was supposed to be him helping her out?

Still, he had five hours to come up with a plan. No problem. Chris juggled the phone in his left hand to end the call and put it away since his right was holding up the garment bag holding his tuxedo and his tote.

Benny and Sydney stopped their quiet discussion when he opened the door. "Sorry about that. I had to take a call."

"Anything wrong?"

"No, not at all," he lied.

Sydney checked her watch and cocked her head the same way his sister did when she was doing mental arithmetic. "We should get started. Do you want to put the tux back in your car?"

"Aren't we all going? You said that we needed to run some errands this morning."

She grinned. "Not for this one. It's just down the street."

Chris laid the garment bag flat on the floor of the trunk and tucked his gym bag against the wheel well. Then he trotted back down the sidewalk behind the striding Sydney, admiring the nape of her neck under the folded up brim of her hat. A few wispy locks had escaped her braid and bounced as she moved. He was so interested he nearly missed the hairpin turn up the walkway three doors down.

Sydney leaned on her neighbor's doorbell.

"You know that it isn't even seven yet. You weren't pleased when I showed up this early on a Saturday."

She waggled her finger at him. "That was almost an hour ago. Besides, I'm expected." She leaned on the buzzer again.

Chris swore he heard the staccato of paw nails on tile, but there was no barking from the other side of the door. "Why are we harassing your neighbor so early?"

Now he heard footsteps.

"I'm not harassing them. You are." Sydney ducked behind him as the door opened from the inside.

A gray-haired lady in a lime green bathrobe and matching walking cast stared at him. "Who the hell are you?" she asked as she stroked a monstrous black cat she cradled in her arms.

Twice in one morning? He was going to get a complex. "My name is Chris Peck."

"Hi, Betty. He's here to walk Odin," Sydney offered from behind him.

"Who's Odin?" he asked over his shoulder.

Betty held the cat out to him. "This is Odin, the all-father of the Norse gods, ruler of Valhalla."

Behind him, Sydney snorted. "You know. A fellow king of the gods."

"Hello, Odin. I am Zeus, king of the Greek gods and ruler of Mount Olympus." He reached out to scratch the cat's head. It hissed at him.

Now he heard a belly laugh.

Betty pressed the cat to his chest. "Hold him while I go get his leash." The woman hobbled a few steps down the hall and stuck her head into her front closet. All Chris could see was a bright green cast off to one side and her neon ass sticking out as he tried to keep from dropping the cat.

"You did this on purpose," he whispered.

"I wouldn't make my worst enemy look at that," Sydney replied.

"I meant the cat thing."

"You said you liked cats. Benny will get a couple pictures of you walking Odin. I'll stand in the background supervising. When we tell people the name of the cat, everyone will have a good laugh."

"It will be humiliating."

"You are my slave for the day, Mr. Peck, and I'm doing you a favor. At worst this is mildly embarrassing and highly entertaining. It's nowhere near humiliating. Besides, karma is a bitch, and I have no intention of pissing her off today. If we have to do this stunt, we'll keep it clean, fun, and short. Now walk the damn cat."

Betty returned holding a neon lime leash, which she attached to Odin's collar while Chris held it still. "Thanks a lot for doing this, hun," she said. To Sydney.

"No problem, Betty. We'll have the all-father back in about half an hour."

Chris set the cat on the stairs and gave the leash a tug. "Come on, cat."

They were close to the end of the block when Sydney stopped again. "What's up?"

"I have to pick up the Jeffersons' dog."

"You take a dog and a cat for a walk at the same time?" That sounded ill-advised.

"Now you know why I'm letting you help. Normally, I just walk Polk in the mornings, but when Betty hurt her foot, I ended up with Odin too."

"Polk?"

"Named after the president. The Jeffersons are very patriotic."

"I'll walk the dog instead of mighty Odin here," Chris offered.

"No, you don't want to do that."

"I really do."

"I realize you may not trust me after the Odin thing, but believe me when I say you are better off walking the cat."

"Please let me keep a shred of my dignity and have the dog," Chris pleaded.

Sydney stared at him and shook her head. "No. Now stop. Stay."

This was taking a joke too far. What would it hurt to let him walk the dog? Yes, the cat would make a better picture, but he still had his image to maintain. No romantic comedy male lead had walked a cat in any movie ever. He was supposed to be able to use today to help his career, not tank it. He wondered if it would make a difference if he offered cash for the chance to walk Polk.

Then he saw the dog. Chris could barely stop himself from falling down and worshipping at Sydney's feet. He'd keep the cat. He loved Odin. Gods like them belonged together. He would walk the fine specimen of a feline with pride and absolute pleasure.

At least Odin was recognizable as a cat.

Polk was a poodle. A white toy poodle. Polk was a white toy poodle with a turquoise Mohawk, a scarlet heart dyed in the center of her back, and a rhinestone-studded collar. Red, white, and blue was supposed to be patriotic. The dog was visual terrorism. It took a moment for Chris' gaze to move past the monstrosity of the dog itself, but he eventually spotted the dog's heinous rainbow-sequined leash. "What is that?"

Sydney stopped halfway down the sidewalk while the dog squatted on the front lawn. "This is Polk. Would you like to trade?"

"God, no! I mean, you're the boss today, and you said that I had to walk Odin so that is exactly what I'm going to do. I'm walking the cat."

"Can't you be bribed?" She smiled at him and pulled her arm out from behind her back. "Polk comes with her own pooper scooper," she teased. Sydney held out a little bedazzled shovel with a plastic baggie tied over the spade end, and an empty baggie tied to the handle.

Chris couldn't back away fast enough. He could hear Benny squeezing off frame after frame, but that was the least of his worries at the moment. Holy hell, she was trying to give him a pooper scooper. Chris got his feet caught in the leash that Odin had twined around his ankles while he was momentarily blinded by the sparkling collar. He almost executed a face plant into the sidewalk before Sydney caught his arm. "I'll keep the cat."

"Thought so."

She held her head up high as she led the way to the park. Benny ran ahead to get a better angle of the two of them walking by. From his grins, he got some good shots.

"Do you have what you need?" Chris asked the photographer.

"Yeah, I've got some really good stuff already."

Chris pointed to some empty picnic tables at the park's entrance. "Why don't you get them all transferred and uploaded while we walk? I don't think anything else is going to happen." He turned to check with Sydney. "Is anything else going to happen while we're here?"

"No, I think the animals will keep us busy enough. It takes about twenty minutes to go around the park. I usually make one circuit and then take them back home. Does that work for you, Benny?"

"That'll give me enough time to get all this done. We'll meet back here when you're done?"

"Twenty minutes," Sydney confirmed.

They passed the play structure in the far corner of the park before either of them spoke again.

"This is awkward," Sydney said quietly.

"It doesn't have to be."

"You're a movie star. What could we have to talk about?"

"How did you phrase it before? Pretend I'm a normal person," Chris suggested. He wanted this morning to work. If she were uncomfortable around him, it would be bad for everyone involved. It would also make the photo shoot incredibly awkward. It went beyond the job issue, though. Sydney really was doing him a huge favor, and she was doing it without embarrassing him. She was right when she said the cat setup was funny and clean. She could have done so much worse to him, and she hadn't. She'd even gotten him out of the penguin suit. The very least he could do was make it as painless as possible. His life coach would be proud.

"We can't pretend this is like a date. Terms of service, remember. Not to mention, you're legally required to be here," she protested.

"Think of it like a blind date set up by my boss. Nothing's going to happen, but we can still have some fun."

They strolled a bit farther in silence before she nodded. "I can do that. A pretend date. So now that we've introduced ourselves, we go on to the next part of the first date conversation?"

"Exactly."

Sydney looked up at him with the same devious look she had when right before she'd introduced him to Betty and Odin. Her eyes sparkled under the brim of her hat. Evil was looking pretty damn attractive this morning. Then she spoke. "So, Chris, what do you do for a living?"

Oh, he liked this girl.

Chapter 4

After a disastrous start, the morning was turning out pretty well. She hadn't gotten all the sleep she was going to need to get through the day, but the animals were walked and returned to their homes and she was in a limousine on her way to her next stop before the clock hit eight. Even in a private car, the ride was still more than half an hour. It was faster than the bus, but getting to the other side of Los Angeles took time.

While Chris gave her directions to the driver and then had a whispered conversation with the photographer, Sydney pulled out her phone and sent a flurry of texts. God, her friends were great. They were already up and running after a sake Friday night and were headed out on their various assignments. She put her phone away and began playing with the switches on the panel on the backseat armrest. Sydney didn't notice anything happening until a sunbeam hit her square in the eye. She squinted despite the sunglasses she wore. "I found the moon roof controls." She flicked the tab until the roof closed again. She spared her pseudo-date a glance from behind the shaded lenses. "What? I haven't been in one of these before." She tried a dial. Rap music blared from the speakers behind her head. "Off. Off!" She was running out of buttons.

Chris leaned over, and the nasty sounds disappeared. "What do you think?"

"I was kind of expecting a panel that popped out holding bottles of scotch and champagne and crystal glasses," she admitted.

"That is more for the larger limos. We didn't ask for one of those. Sorry."

She shrugged. "It's eight in the morning. It's not like

I would have drunk it anyway. The driver knows which grocery store I meant, right? The one on the corner of…"

"He knows." Chris opened the sunroof again. "Do you mind some fresh air?"

Sydney leaned back into the soft leather seat. The sun hit her chest, warming it. "I don't mind."

She wasn't as relaxed as she was pretending to be. Since this was supposed to be a first date, that was to be expected. She wouldn't be completely relaxed on a first date, either. She looked at the bench on the side of the limo. Benny sat quietly, his camera in his lap, waiting for the next photo opportunity.

Chris looked totally at ease. She studied him out of the corner of her eye, keeping her glasses pointed straight ahead. She could do casual. She'd be faking like a bitch, and it might actually kill her, but she could pull it off. Sydney envied the way he stretched out, comfortable in his own skin even when he was among strangers. She was also a little jealous of his shirt. She'd been right earlier. He did have the six-pack and arms to match that she thought were hiding under the tuxedo jacket. His slacks were also snug in all the right places. He didn't have the bulging muscle physique going on. He looked more like a runner. She'd dated runners before. They didn't have the same brute strength as weight lifters, but they sure as hell had better stamina.

"Why are we going to a grocery store way up in Glendale?" Chris asked.

"Because I have a special order to pick up. Besides, this way I can embarrass you in another part of town."

"I can't wait."

Speaking of arrangements, Sydney pulled a fat, spiral-bound notebook out of her purse. Her phone was great, but some things needed paper. The dog-walking had moved up half an hour, and the ride to the grocery store put her an hour and thirty-three minutes ahead of schedule, giving her a whole thirteen minutes immediately available for fun. She took a deep breath and returned the notebook to its zippered pocket in her purse. She hadn't planned for time to breathe today. Now she'd knock a couple more items off her to-do list and be home with time to spare before lunch.

She adjusted herself in the leather seat. The limo was cool. She was in a limo with a movie star who was spending the morning with her. Unglamorous Sydney was getting a taste of the high life. She liked it. Yes, it was temporary, and yes, the entire situation was manufactured. It didn't take away from the cool factor. She had a gorgeous man who was at hand and trapped with her for almost fifteen minutes. If it were real it would put her over the top, but she'd happily settle for pretend. For a day that was supposed to be from hell, she couldn't fake blasé in the face of its awesomeness.

Despite the fresh air, the politeness in the back of the limousine was stifling. Sydney hoped she and Chris would find some common ground soon, even if their time together was almost over. "Going back to the conversation we started at the park, what do you do when you're not acting or being someone's slave for the day?" she asked.

"What?"

"What do you do for fun? Do you surf? Do you enter barbecue cook-offs with your own secret sauce recipe? Do you hide in your basement and translate the Harry Potter books into Sumerian? Do you…"

"Stop, please! You have a scary imagination. I hike. I'm hoping to hit every state park by the end of next year."

"How many parks have you visited already?"

"Over a hundred."

"Damn, that's a lot of parks." She'd almost called it. Hiking was better than walking, but not quite the same as running. Sydney liked walking. She'd done a lot of walking trails in the city. She'd never tried an honest-to-God hiking path though. It sounded like a lot of work, but she'd bet the views were worth it.

"I'm taking a photography course. Landscapes," she offered in return. She'd started with taking pictures out her window, then graduated to local parks and beaches. After some trial and error, she learned she did not have an architect's eye. Her building shots always looked like the structure was about to fall over. For a time she'd tried to find dilapidated structures for subjects so it wouldn't matter. Those shots didn't turn out either. She did better in the natural world.

"You have to go to Castle Crags up in Shasta. It's not a long hike, but the scenery is amazing."

"Cool. Any other favorites?"

Chris smirked. "All of them. After California I'd love to do all of the state and national parks in Hawaii."

"I've been to Hawaii," she said. "I did the bike ride around Diamond Head. It was awesome."

"You are up on me then. I haven't been to the fiftieth state at all."

"You should go. It's a short flight from Los Angeles. I went in the off season with some friends after my sophomore year at college."

Chris looked at Benny, who was paying attention to their conversation. He leaned over and whispered. "I'm not a big flier."

Sydney felt her eyebrows rise above her sunglasses' frames. "Really?"

The actor nodded. "Uh-huh."

She was feeling a little naughty after the rush of warm breath in her ear. She leaned toward him. "So you'd take a cruise ship there and back?" she whispered back.

"I think I could handle a plane if I had a pretty distraction," he murmured. His breath tickled the hairs that had fallen onto her neck.

Her cheeks began to burn. She didn't even know if he was flirting with her or stating a fact.

Screw it. Terms of service be damned. He was flirting. It was Valentine's Day, and she hadn't had a date since February of last year, and Chris was hot and successful and a screen idol worshipped by millions of women, and right now he was all hers. If she was going to pretend that this was a date then she was going to pretend hard enough to believe it and forget the repercussions until they slapped her upside the head, as they no doubt would. Dragging her date along as she completed a list of errands wasn't the most romantic date she'd had, but it was all she had. Unfortunately, it wasn't the worst date she'd ever had. She had never returned to Dick's in Las Vegas or seen the guy who'd taken her there again.

They took a tight left turn and immediately slowed as they jolted over a speed bump at the entrance to the grocery store. The limo stopped in front of the main doors.

Sydney didn't move. Everyone in the parking lot was staring at them. Perhaps this wasn't the best idea.

"Sydney, we're here."

"Everyone is staring at us."

"I know. It's okay."

"I hate people staring at me. They're going to take

pictures." Sydney looked over at Benny. "Sorry, no offense." She despised photos. There was a time when she would have posed with a smile without a second thought. She'd had her fifteen minutes of fame since then. It wasn't pleasant, and she didn't want to repeat it; experience was a good teacher.

He reached across the console, took her hand, and gave it a squeeze. "It's okay. Just fake it. If it gets really bad, I'll cause a distraction. I'll take off my shirt or something." He grinned at her, obviously fishing for a smile back.

She tried, but it felt like more of a grimace. He was great looking and sensitive. Of course he was perfect—he was from Hollywood. Where was his alter ego for the women like her who lived in the real world? If she could find someone like that in Norwalk, she wouldn't need to go to the movies ever again.

"If you want, we can send the car away while we're inside," Chris continued.

Yes, please, let's do that. "No, if we need to make a quick getaway we need it close by." Besides, the limo was only inconvenient now. In half an hour it was going to give her a fantastic entrance and make someone's day.

He was still holding her hand. She squeezed back. "Let's do this. It should only take a few minutes." She waited for Chris to open the door, but he didn't. She scooted down the seat, and he still didn't move. Then the door opened from the outside. Oh, yeah. She'd forgotten about the driver.

Chris got out first. Then he helped her out of the car. Sydney was glad she'd tucked her recycled grocery bags inside her purse. She held her breath as they walked into the store. She could do this.

She pointed to the dairy cooler along the wall. "Let's start there."

Chapter 5

Chris knew shoppers. He'd gone baby furniture shopping with his pregnant, hormonal sister. He'd gone shoe shopping with various girlfriends. He'd gone electronics shopping with his co-star Nick Thurston when they'd each bought a new home entertainment system after being picked up for a second season. Now he understood they were all amateurs. Sydney was a shopper. The woman had a precise list and a disconcerting sense of direction. And she could move. They'd be done inside of twenty-five minutes, including checkout time, if he didn't kill himself first.

She wasn't being a bitch driving him toward suicide. His death would be completely accidental. It had taken him forever to pull the grocery cart out of the row of death contraptions. And that was after he realized he had to insert a quarter to disconnect the locking mechanism on the chain. When he finally got the cart free, he yanked the handles right into his stomach and knocked the wind out of himself. Then he had to run to catch up as Sydney zipped up and down the aisles.

Two single quart containers of milk. One container of Greek yogurt. Two tins of sardines and a box of Ritz crackers. Two cases of high calcium meal replacement shakes. Men's deodorant. Lavender hand soap. Chris didn't think it was possible for Sydney's list to be more eclectic.

He was spending too much time looking in the cart and not enough time looking where it was going. That's what he told himself when he rammed the cart into the back of Sydney's ankle when she stopped dead in the middle of the aisle. It had nothing to do with the sway of her hips as he followed her around.

"Sorry. I'm sorry, are you okay?" He was so smooth. Maybe if he crippled her badly enough she wouldn't be able to run away when he sprang the photo shoot on her later. It was his best plan to date.

"Fine."

"Why did we stop?"

"You can't go any farther."

"Why not?"

Sydney waved at the display in front of her. There were trays of heart-shaped cakes and cookies and sprinkle-covered cupcakes. "I am not putting a wheat-starved man in the position of being tempted. In fact, maybe you should move back a bit so the smells don't weaken your resolve."

The sweet, yeasty scents in the air hadn't bothered him until she pointed them out. God, he missed carbs. Usually it was only the thought of pasta that caused his stomach to growl, but the fresh bread being rolled out of the bakery was doing serious damage to his self-control. He backed up a couple steps.

Sydney bypassed all the Valentine's Day tables and headed right to the cake counter. She pulled a slip of paper from her wallet and handed it to the tiny woman behind the giant glass display case. The woman disappeared for a few minutes and returned with two tin trays with plastic shells covering them. She placed a sticker on each lid and handed them to Sydney, who balanced them carefully as she walked back to the cart. She put her precious cargo in the kiddie seat, where Chris was finally able to see what she was carrying. Individual cakes decorated in white frosting with red piped icing spelling out "Happy Valentine's Day, Gran" and "Happy Valentine's Day" respectively, with a "prepaid" sticker on each of them.

"You're shopping for two different people," Chris blurted in comprehension. The cart contents made so much more sense. Now he could see the split between the items. He took a second look inside the cart and shook his head. There was an actual divide in the items. Sydney had been placing them on different ends of the cart as she'd loaded it up. Thank God he wasn't playing a detective.

"I am. But they are at the same location so it's only one stop. Come on, I'll stop your torture soon. But first, we get fruit!" She grabbed the front of the cart and spun it until it faced the other direction.

He ripped bag after bag off the roll at the banana stand and handed them to Sydney, who darted all over the produce aisle. Chris held the first one loosely in one hand as he tried to separate the layers and open it for the waiting tomatoes. Not only were the damn things practically ironed together, the static between them also upped the difficulty level when it came to opening them. It took him two tries to realize he was working on the wrong end. He barely kept up to her commands of "open" and "tie" as she filled them with fresh oranges and peppers. Her hands were full of grapes when she spotted a pile of melons two stands over.

"Chris, can you grab a couple of cantaloupes for me, please? And give them a squeeze to make sure they are mostly ripe? Thanks."

He could do that. He ate melons. He knew the firmness Sydney was talking about, the one between stones and mush. He pawed through the pile and came up with two acceptable specimens.

"How are those cantaloupes coming?" Sydney asked as she came around the corner, holding a bag. Chris held them out victoriously. She took one look at him and immediately whipped around. "Put those down! Where's

Benny?"

Chris dropped them into a crate of Mackintosh apples. "He's picking out a candy bar. Why? What's wrong?"

"Look, I said I wouldn't purposely put you in any humiliating pictures today, but I can't help you if you set yourself up."

"What are you talking about?"

"Where were you holding those melons?"

Chris started to raise his hands to their previous positions when Sydney grabbed his wrists and forced his forearms back down.

"Just tell me," she instructed.

"In front of me, chest high," he said.

"You were holding melons up in front of your chest?"

"Yes." What was her problem?

"You were holding and squeezing two melons in front of your chest?" she repeated slowly.

"Yes, what's your...?" Oh, crap. Yeah, that could have been bad. And the guys at The Source owed him one after he blocked a potentially embarrassing shot of a commando Nick in a soaking wet toga last month. There'd been an incident on the set. "Thanks."

"No problem. Now, please hand me the cantaloupes one at a time."

Her timing was spectacular. Benny came back as he dropped the second one in the bag and got a shot of him pushing a full cart toward the cashiers. He got another set of photos as Chris loaded the bags back into the cart. The cashier handed Sydney her receipt and a gas coupon, and then handed a second coupon to Benny. Chris couldn't make out the details, but there was definitely a name and phone number written on the back. The intern seemed pleased.

"I thought purple was more your type. She's a blonde," Chris noted as they unloaded the groceries into the trunk. He'd already moved his tux to the passenger seat beside the driver.

"So what? She was cute."

He waited for Sydney to give instructions to the driver and then helped her into the back of the limo. Her palm was warm in his, and he held it a little longer than was necessary, but she didn't say anything so he didn't either. He thought about holding on as she slid across the seat, but Benny was right behind him. Besides, that was date behavior, and this was anything but, no matter how pretty he found her.

Chris settled in beside her and smiled back when she beamed at him. "Don't worry, you are almost a free man. Mr. Banks is going to drop me off, and then you're done."

It was a little past nine. She wasn't going to disappear on him already. She couldn't. He must have heard wrong. "Excuse me?"

"Mr. Banks, the driver? He's going to drop me at my grandmother's seniors' complex. And then you have fulfilled your obligations for the sweepstakes. Thanks for the ride. I really appreciate it. I can get myself home by noon from here."

She was serious. She was going to cut him loose after a few minor errands and a handful of photos. Sydney wasn't going to try to force him to stay beyond what he was required to, or show off her slave to her friends, or put him through any of the horrible situations he and his castmates had come up with the night before. And she was making it sound as if he did her the favor.

"No, I'm not done with you yet." She couldn't leave him in the lurch. Martine said the show's production company was going all out for the on-set reception. Other people had been invited. Important people. She hadn't named names, but there was a money connection between Olympus and High Note Productions. The movie people might be checking him out directly. She hadn't said it in so many words, but it was possible.

He needed Sydney—er, this—badly. Casting announcements were expected next week, and this was his last chance to demonstrate he could woo a woman without a toga. She had to come back to the studio. That's the type of thing karma would reward him with for starring in this circus.

Not that it was horrible. Chris liked Sydney and her normal life. He used to be good at normal, and it was a nice change. She was nice. He wasn't ready to part ways so quickly. He was an actor; he should be able to talk her into sticking around for a while. He'd charmed hundreds of fans at conventions and red carpet events. He had to be able to put out enough charisma to sweet talk Sydney.

A cute, confused look flashed across her face. "Why not? Benny got all kinds of pictures, right?" She looked at the teenager sitting across from her. "You did, right?"

"I got some good ones. I need to upload the grocery store shots though."

Sydney turned back to face him. "See? The world has seen you fetching my coffee and walking my cat. You're golden, Zeus."

She wasn't kidding. She was trying to get rid of him. Which would be great except that he needed her. "We can help you with the groceries and then give you a ride home."

"No, it's okay."

"I can't leave you here. Come on, let me carry the groceries up to your grandmother's place. You'll have your hands full with the cakes anyway."

"I said no. However unwittingly, I volunteered for this spectacle. She didn't. Look, this is my private life. I'm not going to drag my grandma into this."

"What if we leave Benny in the car?" Chris suggested.

"Excuse me?" the photographer said. "You can't leave me behind."

Chris knew where he was coming from. The intern was trying to get into the studio's PR department as a paid photographer. The sweepstakes project was the kid's big shot. Unfortunately, if it came down to Chris using today for a shot at a role and an intern going for a job, Chris was going to pull rank. Benny wouldn't lose the intern slot, but nobody would be offering him a full-time position.

"There was a four paragraph section in the sweepstakes' disclosure document authorizing images and such. My grandma didn't sign it, so you couldn't use her anyway," Sydney told them.

"I have releases in my bag," Benny insisted.

Great, he got the prepared intern. "The lady doesn't want pictures. So we don't take pictures."

"Maybe we could ask your grandma," Benny said directly to Sydney. "Who knows? Maybe she'll want to be in a magazine."

"She's been in magazines," Sydney muttered under her breath. Benny was too far away to hear her, but Chris made out the words.

"Sydney, is your grandmother famous?" he asked.

"Famous. Notorious. Same thing. Speaking of, can I get a bit of privacy while I call her?"

"Sure. You know, if you let us hang around, we can give you a ride home afterwards. It's no problem at all," he added as a last second incentive. It would be interesting to see how far they could push the car advantage. He needed the time to think of another reason for Sydney to stay.

Chris hopped over to the bench beside Benny and herded him up to the driver's privacy window while Sydney pulled a cell phone out of her purse. He made use of the opportunity and kept his voice down. "Benny, don't push too hard on the pictures, okay? You'll get lots, I promise."

"Martine texted me while you were in the store. How come Sydney hasn't mentioned the shoot on the set? She's talking about going home," Benny whispered back.

"I haven't told her about that yet."

"What?"

Chris waved his hand at Sydney, who looked up from her phone. Nothing to see here. We aren't plotting against you or anything, honest. She went back to her call. Apparently she wasn't completely immune to his charms. That was good to know. It was a shame he was lying.

"She'll say yes."

"I hope so. I hear Layla's planning a big surprise for when you show up."

"Fantastic." He didn't need to hear that. The actress who played Hera would not hesitate to throw someone under the bus to gain more popularity points with the show's audience. Layla Andrews was a grade-A bitch with the chops to get away with it because she was that good. However, good and well-liked were not always synonymous in this town. Right now he had a slight edge over her when it came to set politics, and he liked it that way. He didn't know what she had planned, but if she managed to turn the tables on him by messing up this assignment it could be a very long thirteen episodes. Now not only did he absolutely have to get Sydney to the set and agree to do the shoot, he also had to watch her back and his own.

"Okay." Sydney patted the seat beside her. "You can meet my grandma. But she says no photos because her hair's not done and she hasn't put on her makeup yet."

"Fair enough."

They bounced a bit while the limo rolled over the speed bumps in the turnaround outside the seniors' complex. It was a white stucco building about six stories high. It seemed nice and clean from the outside. It wasn't expensive by any stretch. It looked comfortable, like so many things about Sydney's life were.

She waved to a faceless figure in one of the upper windows when he helped her out of the limo. Benny took a series of photos as they unloaded the trunk and headed into the building. Chris held the doors and the large stuffed cloth bags while Sydney balanced the smaller one holding the cakes. He was content to follow her lead as they took the elevator to the fourth floor. When she knocked on the apartment door, it opened almost immediately.

An ancient Marilyn Monroe greeted him with, "Hello, you cheating son of a bitch."

Chapter 6

Sydney slapped her hand over her eyes. She couldn't watch this train wreck. Her grandmother had sounded okay when she'd explained the changes to this morning's schedule. In fact, Nana had made all the right noises about being excited about Sydney winning the Olympus sweepstakes and about getting the chance to meet Zeus himself.

She should have known the old lady had other motives.

Her grandmother was an ardent television watcher. Her biggest expense was her monthly cable bill, since she got every specialty station available. In fact, it was Nana who had introduced her to Olympus in the first place. She adored the show. Sydney hadn't expected her to blur the lines between television and reality.

She snuck a peek at Chris. He stood stock-still outside the door. Sydney assumed it was because of the insult, but then she noticed he was trying to speak. He seemed to be stuttering over the letter "M". Crap, she forgot to warn him about that part.

"It's not what you think," she whispered to him.

"Really? Because I'm thinking that the reason your grandmother doesn't want to be photographed is because she doesn't want people to know that Marilyn Monroe has been hiding in Glendale for the last fifty years."

"Nana, may I present Mr. Chris Peck, who plays 'Zeus' on the TV show Olympus. Chris, this is my grandmother, Helen Richardson, who was one of Marilyn's unofficial publicity doubles from back in the day."

Chris set down a bag of groceries and stuck out his hand. "It's nice to meet you, ma'am."

"I can't believe you slept with Demeter. That actress who plays Hera is so lovely, all black hair and chocolate eyes. It's not very gentlemanly of you to cheat."

Sydney refused to look up again. Her not-date was getting an ethics lesson from the woman who used to make a living pretending to be someone else.

"In my defense, I am the king of the gods. Zeus sleeps with everyone. And she did try to kill me in episode nine."

Her grandmother gave this due consideration. "That might make me a little tetchy too. Cheating's still not right."

"It never is, ma'am."

"Well, don't stand in the hall. Come in," she said. "Then you can tell me all the twists coming up this season."

Shoot me now, Sydney thought. She picked up the bag Chris left in the hall when her grandma grabbed his free hand and pulled him into her little living room. Sydney was relieved to see it was tidy with nothing embarrassing on display. The complex offered bi-weekly housekeeping so it never got completely out of hand. Tidy wasn't the problem. There wasn't a big enough bucket of brain bleach to get rid of the image of Nana's apartment the day she had a lingerie party. The ladies attending were completely clothed, but even the idea of them in those clothes had turned Sydney off pushup bras for the duration.

Chris shot her a confused look from the living room, but she ignored him. She hadn't wanted him to come up in the first place. He'd insisted. Now he could deal with a feisty ninety-year-old while she unpacked the groceries in the kitchenette.

The fridge was in good shape. Sydney tossed the few

shriveling grapes from last week's bag and put the new bunch in the crisper. There was no yogurt at all in the fridge, which meant that either Grandma's calcium was up or that she left it on the counter and it went bad so she'd thrown it out. Sydney would have to ask what happened.

"Nana, would you like some cake and coffee?" she called from the kitchen.

"That would be lovely, sweetie. Mr. Peck, would you like to join us?"

"He can't," Sydney said. She popped the lid off the cake and carried it into the living room. She set it on the coffee table and turned it so the holiday message was visible.

"Sydney, don't you think you are taking the 'slave' thing a little too far?" the old lady warned.

"Yeah, Sydney," Chris said. "I'm your slave. The least you could do is feed me."

"No cake for you. You can have coffee."

"Sydney!" Nana admonished.

He was getting her in trouble with her own grandmother. She should have left him in the limo with Benny. "I let you walk the cat!" she said to Chris.

"That's probably not helping your argument at this point," he replied with a smirk.

"Nana, Chris is on a diet. He can't have flour so he doesn't get any cake. And if he keeps this up he's not going to get any coffee either. Do you get me, Zeus?"

Chris snickered, and Nana laughed out loud. Then she reached over and slapped Chris on the knee a couple times and squeezed. Chris froze when the old lady's hand made contact with his thigh. Then Sydney started laughing. It served the Greek god right. She wasn't allowed to touch per the "I Agree" button she'd clicked.

Her grandmother hadn't, so let him fight her off. She was so far past cougar she was probably a saber-toothed tiger.

Sydney made a couple more trips and returned with two plates and forks and a tray of coffee and cups. She handed Chris' coffee to him and took the opportunity to whisper in his ear. "Keep it up and you'll be serving me, toga boy." The blush on his face was worth the fact that she couldn't breathe. Sydney couldn't believe she'd said that. Hello, Miss Forward and Flirting. Nice to see you again.

It felt pretty good too. She'd forgotten she even knew how.

She listened to her grandma wheedle away unsuccessfully as Chris refused to give any hints on upcoming storylines for the show. Sydney loved her family, but it was hard being the one who came to visit and check up on her grandmother every week. It was easy to run out of things to talk about, especially considering the number of topics they couldn't discuss.

Sydney glanced at her watch. She wasn't worried about falling behind since she had the limo at her disposal, but she did have another stop to make. She got up and began moving the used dishes into the little stainless-steel sink. It was a matter of minutes to clean them up. She cracked open the cupboard door under the sink to hang the damp dish towel on the edge of it. The door was swinging closed when she caught it and opened it again.

"Where's your fire extinguisher, Nana?"

"Under the sink, dear."

"No, it's not." A quick search revealed it was not under the sink, or in any of the cupboards or in the tiny broom closet. Sydney checked the hall closet and the bathroom, and there was still no sign of it. "Nana, where did you put it?"

Sydney could hear the woman trailing around behind her. "Don't worry, dear. It's here somewhere."

"Somewhere is not going to help when you need it."

"Sydney, dear, I don't even have a stove."

"Right, because that's the only way fires start. Accidents happen to other people," Sydney snapped. Jesus, they had this argument at least once a month. How hard was it to leave a fire extinguisher under the kitchen sink? Nana didn't have to go under there for anything else. All she had to do was leave it under there in case there was an emergency. But no, that would make too much sense.

Sydney pressed her lips together and held her breath. Her lungs fought against her restraint, but she absolutely refused to fall into another panic attack. The extinguisher was missing, but there wasn't a fire. It wasn't like that night in the house when Nana had put a grilled cheese sandwich in the pan and then went back into the living room and got caught up in the news broadcast.

There was no fire.

Chris caught her arm as she stormed into the bedroom. "Sydney, your grandmother is crying."

"Tears won't put out a fire. Believe me. She needs to stop doing this." She shrugged him off and dropped to the floor, looking under the bed skirt and behind the dresser. She found the red cylinder tucked inside a lone cowboy boot. Sydney hauled both of them out from under the bed and set them on the duvet. "Really, Grandma?"

Nana's watery eyes didn't move her. They'd lost their effects after the first three times they'd played this game. "I'm sorry, sweetheart. I needed to stretch out the leather at the ankle."

"Just leave it under the sink, Grandma. Please."

Sydney was tempted to push the extinguisher to the far corner, behind the elbow joint. But putting it out of reach would be counterproductive. Instead, she left it against the inside of the cupboard wall, inside just enough that the door could close without knocking it.

She gathered up the now-empty grocery bag and put it back into her purse. She gathered up the second bag, and the one containing the other cake, and stepped up to her grandma. She bent over to give her a gentle hug. "I'll see you next week. Thanks for entertaining Chris for me."

Chris bowed at the waist and kissed the old woman's hand. "It was a pleasure to meet you, Mrs. Richardson."

"You treat my grandbaby well, Zeus."

"I will."

The elevator ride down to the second floor was silent until Chris said, "She didn't mean any harm."

"Let it go."

"I'm trying to help."

"Chris, have I given you any tips on how to act?"

"No."

"Then do me the same courtesy." So much for flirting. Sydney sighed.

Chapter 7

He was the slave. If she told him to shut up, he'd listen. How she treated her family was none of his business. "Where are we going next?"

"Friend."

Great, now they were down to one word answers. This was going to impress the producers. He grabbed the grocery bag automatically when Sydney held it out to him. It seemed he still had a job to do.

He recognized the head toss and shoulder roll as Sydney tried to shake off the episode with her grandmother. It was obvious she wasn't an actress. Her body had released some of the tension he'd seen since she left the elderly woman's apartment, but her smile was so fake it hurt to watch. The spat must have been worse than he knew. And he'd added to it. Now he felt bad.

"Your friend?" he tried again.

"Family friend. He knew Nana back in the day."

She knocked on the door of a corner suite and waited. Eventually, Chris heard some muffled shuffling. The chain slid off the steel runner with a rasp, then clunked against the doorframe. It opened to the heavily lined face of a gray-haired man whom he vaguely recognized, but he couldn't put a name to him.

"Happy Valentine's Day, Mr. Dobson," Sydney said.

That was the name. Gary Dobson was a legend behind the camera. He'd directed the premiere episodes of eight of the top ten shows of the seventies. The fortunate few unknowns he'd replaced in minor roles on his shows had shot to immediate stardom on the big screen. Chris had heard some of the old timers on the lot say the man could tell if a show was going to win the night's ratings just by reading the script. Gary Dobson had a golden touch. When he disappeared from the limelight in the eighties, the Writers Guild of America went on their longest strike in history, effectively crippling the entertainment industry. Of course, the strike wasn't related to him leaving. That anyone could prove.

Now Chris was trying to break out into movies, and he was standing in front of a man who had the knowledge to tell him how to do it. Unfortunately, the woman who could make it happen was pissed at him. This was not how karma was supposed to work. He was sure this day couldn't get worse. He wasn't certain how, but he was sure it was possible.

"Good morning, Sydney. Who's your friend?"

Chris didn't quite elbow Sydney out of his way in his eagerness to get an introduction. "Hello, Mr. Dobson, sir. My name is Chris Peck."

"Chris is an actor," Sydney offered.

"Yes, I gathered that," the old man said. He let Chris pump his hand a few more times before he shook him off. "It's nice to meet you, Chris. Won't you come in?"

The suite was larger and nicer than the last one. There was an extra door, which Chris presumed led to a second bedroom, and it had a full kitchen. He noticed a lack of Hollywood memorabilia, a distinct difference from Mrs. Richardson's place. Her walls were covered with photos of her, or the real Marilyn Monroe, he couldn't tell the difference, at various functions and with a number of who's who from the era. The pictures here were of family and places that looked genuine. They lacked the gloss but had the reality.

By the time he finished his inspection, Sydney and Mr. Dobson were in the kitchen. She was teasing him about the cake.

"You did remember to get Mrs. D something, right?

Flowers? Candy? A card?"

"She's got me. What else does she need?"

"Flowers. Candy. A card," Sydney teased. "Or a cake. Look, you're all set!"

"You are a sweetheart, Sydney. Would you like to say hi to Arlene? She's in the bedroom."

Sydney left, and Chris was alone with the great Gary Dobson. He couldn't think of anything to say.

"I recognize you. From Olympus. Good show."

"Thank you, sir."

"How do you know our Sydney?"

"She won the Olympus sweepstakes. I'm her slave for a day."

"I remember that promotion. Good idea. I thought they could have done more with it though. How did you end up as the slave? Surely there were others that could have done it."

Chris gulped. To lie, or not to lie. That was the question. "Originally I lost a bet but I realized I could make it work for me."

Mr. Dobson laughed. "You got lucky. Sydney is a doll. She won't treat you too badly." He pulled a glass from the cupboard. "Would you like a drink?"

"No, thank you, sir. We had coffee upstairs."

The old man's smile disappeared. "So you met Marilyn. Helen."

"Yes, sir."

"Drop the 'sir', would you?"

"Okay, Mr. Dobson."

Chris flinched under the glare. No wonder the man had a reputation of no messing around on set.

"What did you think of our resident celebrity?"

Now there was a setup. Mr. Dobson was looking for a specific answer. As an actor, Chris should be thinking professionally, and Helen/Marilyn had some serious power to consider. But then he had called Sydney "sweetheart". "She and Sydney had an argument about a fire extinguisher."

"And you said something. That explains the tension between you."

"Her grandmother started crying."

Checking to make sure that Sydney had indeed gone into the bedroom, the elderly gentleman slapped Chris' shoulder. "Without breaking any confidences, I can tell you that Helen and Sydney tried to live together for a time, but Helen needed more supervision than Sydney could provide. There's a reason she's in a suite with no stove."

Chris gulped. "Did she start a fire?" It was the only explanation he could think of that could have triggered Sydney's freak out about the fire extinguisher. It also explained the glassed-in one in Sydney's hall at her house.

"A small one. But there were other near-misses. She had to move out for Sydney's sake." Mr. Dobson swung the door under the sink open. He had an identical extinguisher in exactly the same place Sydney had put her grandmother's. "Our girl is nobody's fool. The point of insurance is not to need it. Keeping that down there costs me nothing, gets me goodwill, and may save my family's life one day. Why would I throw that away to prove that I had more control than a little girl trying to do the right thing?" He eased the door shut silently when he heard voices coming from the next room. "My wife is making an appearance. Would you like to meet her?"

"Yes, sir, Mr. Dobson." Crap. The frown was back.

His wife was a little bit of a thing, bent with age and radiating frailty. Chris couldn't say for certain if he even knew his hero was married. He did a quick review in his head. In every photo he could remember, Gary Dobson was alone or with his cast. He never appeared in public with his family, and nobody ever said anything about it. How the hell could nobody have said anything for thirty-some years?

"Hello, Mrs. Dobson." Chris shook her hand once Sydney had eased her into a recliner in the corner.

"So you're our girl's slave, are you? She was going crazy over the prizes." Her voice was soft and melodic.

Chris liked calling Sydney "our girl". He'd like it better if she were a "his girl". When life got nuts, it would be nice to have someone who was there just for you. He'd bet Sydney would be great at it. "Would you be more impressed if I said I was usually a Greek god but I'm having an off day?"

She laughed. Mr. Dobson laughed. Even Sydney laughed at him, and gave him a smile he took to mean he was forgiven for his comment in the elevator. When Mrs. Dobson's laugh turned into a cough, her husband sprang to her side. Sydney pointed at the kitchenette. "Water. Glasses are beside the sink."

Chris was back in seconds. The elderly woman spilled the water as she took her first sip. "Thank you, Chris. Have you asked my husband your question yet?"

"What question?" Chris sat beside Sydney, who had scooted down to make room for him on the sofa.

"What is the secret to getting the award-winning roles I want? How can I tell from the script if the project will be a hit or a flop? Can I rub your belly for luck like a Buddha?" The white-haired woman snorted. "I wouldn't suggest that last one. It took him almost twenty years to get over it when a soap opera actress asked him."

Oh my God, that answers so many questions. He

glanced toward Sydney and expected to see her laughing at the belly comment as well. She wasn't. She sported a smile, but the look in her eyes was more resigned than amused. And she too was waiting for his question.

She was waiting for him to take advantage. He'd pretty much forced her to let him tag along or risk being left at the other end of town. And now he was going to use her personal connection to someone she'd likely never used on her own to advance his career. She certainly was lucky he was her slave for the day. Imagine how much he might have missed out on if he hadn't been along to help her out. He could practically hear his life coach screaming in his ear so he took a minute to think.

It wasn't as if he'd ever see her again after the contest. Yes, he could be an arrogant SOB, but he hadn't quite crossed that line yet. Was it that important to him when he already had the opportunity lined up? "Actually, I do have a question. Is Sydney a cyborg? I mean, have you seen her in a store? The woman must be part machine."

Mr. Dobson inhaled the coffee he'd picked up from the end table. Chris jumped up and rescued the water glass from Mrs. Dobson before she dropped it as she rocked in laughter. Sydney's reaction was the best though. Her chin dropped, and she stared at him with the most incredulous expression.

The look was worth passing up the chance to ask a legend for advice. It was a genuine response to him. He'd forgotten what that was like. He couldn't keep an answering grin off his face.

"We made the mistake of asking Sydney to come along when we went linen shopping on Black Friday a couple years ago," Mr. Dobson began.

"Oh, God," Chris interrupted.

"You have no idea. She got behind Arlene's wheelchair and was gone. When we got home, Arlene asked if we could weld on a grill guard to protect her."

"Excuse me, I'm sitting right here." Sydney giggled. Literally giggled. "I didn't hear you complaining when you got those flannel sheets at seventy-five percent off."

"They are good sheets, Gary," his wife agreed.

"Thank you, Arlene. Would you like some cake?"

"If you don't mind, we'll save it for later."

"I don't mind. I already sampled Nana's."

"Chris said there was an incident with the fire extinguisher?" Mr. Dobson fished. Chris dropped his head. He was going to end up back in the doghouse. It would be his fastest return trip ever.

"There's always an incident with that thing. With any luck, we'll have some news soon about moving her to an assisted living facility."

"We'll keep our fingers crossed for you, sweetheart."

Sydney sat up straight on the sofa, the back cushions almost a foot behind her. "Thanks, I'll take all the luck I can get."

Mrs. Dobson stared at the stack of papers on the coffee table. "There's a calendar under there. Would you pass it to me, please, Mr. Peck?"

Chris slipped a cheese recipe calendar out from under a pile of literary magazines. There was something written on today's box, but the handwriting was too shaky for him to read when it was upside-down.

His hostess tapped the square with her finger. "Today is the big day, is it?"

Sydney nodded. "It is."

"Good luck this afternoon."

"Thank you. We'll crush them like the bugs they are." She raised her fists above her head in victory. "But for now we do have to get going. Happy Valentine's Day."

She gave each of them a peck on the cheek, while Chris shook hands. Mr. Dobson walked them to the door. While Sydney ran back to the kitchen to get her grocery bag, the older gentleman grasped his forearm. "Since you didn't ask, I'll tell you. It was Arlene."

"Sir?"

"She had final say on all my projects. My biggest successes were her picks."

Karmic payback for the win! Holy shit, this stuff really worked. Now he knew the secret to one of the biggest successes in the industry. All he had to do was find his own personal savant. No problem.

"Thank you," he said to Sydney on the elevator ride down to the main floor.

"For what?"

"For introducing me to Gary Dobson."

They stepped off the elevator into the lobby, and Sydney slapped herself on the top of her head.

"Syd?"

"I left my hat in Nana's apartment. I'll be right back." She jumped back into the elevator car before the doors had a chance to close.

Chris was alone for the first time that morning. He finally had a minute to think.

He had nothing.

He still had no clue as to how to get Sydney to agree to give him a few hours at the studio when she obviously had something big planned. Unless he kidnapped her. Unfortunately that wasn't an option. Mostly because he was sure she'd kick his ass if he tried.

But this PR event was big too. For the show. For him. Her grandmother would have definitely told her to do it. Mr. Dobson would have explained how many people were counting on them and that a shitload of money had been invested. He couldn't miss out on this kind of opportunity. Maybe she had stuff to do, but there was no reason she couldn't push it back a bit. Chris could compromise. They'd do the photo shoot and meet the cast, staying just long enough to show the High Note people what he could do; then he'd have the limo drop her off where she needed to go. She'd only be a few minutes late at most.

Sydney was smart, and she'd been great so far. This was a great opportunity for her. Her family and friends would want her to do it if they knew about it. He was doing her a favor. She'd never forgive herself if she missed this opportunity because, as great as she was, she was never going to have another chance to be a Hollywood insider like this again.

She'd agree with him once he told her what was happening. He also got the impression she was stubborn enough to not give him the chance to say a word. And if she wasn't going to let him explain, maybe he shouldn't bother trying. What was that saying: it was better to seek forgiveness than ask permission? Sydney had been nothing but classy from their first, well, second meeting. It wasn't like she was going to throw a tantrum at a schedule change.

It wouldn't be hard. All he needed to do was tell Banks to take a slightly different route for the first part of the drive, and they'd be at the studio before she realized he wasn't taking her home.

She'd thank him for it afterward. She would. Now all he had to do was make it happen.

Chris slipped his cell phone out of his pocket and started to put everything into play. A text to Martine

Peeples to tell her they were en route and their expected arrival time. A text to his agent to let him know he'd be on set if the High Note people wanted to see him in action. And a final text to Nick to ask him to bribe craft services into making sure there was some kind of cake for Sydney. He was springing this on her for her own good, but the surprise would probably go over better with cake.

The elevator dinged again, and Sydney re-emerged holding her hat triumphantly. The limo was waiting at the front door, and Chris held Sydney's hand as he helped her in for what she thought was the last time.

"Home, James, through the park," she said to the driver.

"Which park?"

"Just home," she translated.

Once she was safely inside, Chris whispered the new destination to Banks. The chauffer frowned at the change, but a well-placed c-note changed his mind. He flashed a thumbs-up to Benny as they got settled.

It would be nothing but good memories if he ended the day now, like Sydney wanted him to. If he'd been doing this for himself, Chris figured he'd be karmically screwed for his next half a dozen lifetimes. But since he was doing it for her, it couldn't help but go his way.

It was in the bag.

Chapter 8

Sydney had taken a quick look at her phone in the elevator. The gala volunteers were reporting that setup was complete and the tournament people were already onsite. Her schedule was working.

There was a surprising dearth of texts and emails. She suspected it was because her committee heads had ordered all communications be filtered through them, leaving her free to conduct her symphony of chaos. She loved her friends.

Trusting they would contact her if they had to, Sydney relaxed into the seat and found a new panel of buttons to play with on the ride home. A small screen popped out of a side panel. The car was cool, maybe even worth introducing Chris to her family for. She flicked a switch at the end of the panel, and the back of the limo filled with the sound of the most recent, played-non-stop pop monstrosity.

Crap. "Off. Off!" She returned the switch to its original position, and the music stopped. She was improving. Then she realized that it stopped because Chris had turned it off when he answered his phone.

"Hey, Martine," he greeted his caller. "Yeah, we're in the limo now." He listened for a moment and then spoke again. "I'll ask." Chris covered the speaker and looked at Sydney. "Martine, the show's PR person, is on the line. She'd like to ask you a few questions for our contest site."

Sydney shrugged. She'd had a good time, and she was almost home. If they wanted to interview her it would have to be now. "I guess that was part of the package I agreed to, wasn't it?"

"Pretty much. We can use your image, you'll agree

to do some promotional stuff, yadda, yadda, yadda," Chris confirmed. "Can you give her a couple minutes?"

"Sure."

Chris flicked the call onto speaker. "Okay, Martine, we're here."

"Hi, Miss Richardson. I'm Martine Peeples. How's your morning been?"

Sydney leaned forward. "Well, Ms. Peeples, we started off a bit rough, but I put Chris to work as soon as I could."

The woman on the phone with the lovely melodic voice laughed. "I've seen that you're not afraid to get him down and dirty. And please call me Martine."

"Benny's been pretty quick on the draw with his camera," Sydney agreed.

"Can you tell us something that we haven't seen yet?"

"The groceries we picked up were for my grandmother, who requested that she not be photographed. One thing I'll never forget will be watching Chris squirm as she tried to weasel some spoilers for upcoming episodes out of him. He was so cruel. He didn't let a single one slip."

"Hey!" Chris protested.

Sydney shushed him.

"Has he given you any hints of what's to come?" Martine asked.

"He hasn't said anything, but I'm guessing there are going to be a few epic fight scenes this season, but that's pure conjecture on my part based on a couple comments that may not have been in context," Sydney rambled.

"What about past episodes? Which one is your favorite?" Martine asked.

Sydney pinched her lips together. She wasn't so

much of a fan that she'd memorized the first season.

"Give her a second, Martine, she's thinking," Chris said.

"I know! The one where Zeus tells Aphrodite she has to marry Hephaestus. Love, war, and a wedding—all in the same episode." Yes, it was one of her delicious FBI-guy's guest episodes, but they didn't need to know why she picked it.

Chris got progressively quieter as Martine asked her about how her friends reacted to the news and if she knew how many entries she'd won against. His biggest reaction came when the woman was signing off the call.

"This was great, Sydney, thank you. I look forward to meeting you," Martine said.

Chris terminated the call before Sydney could say good-bye.

"Meeting me?" she asked him.

Chris skipped seats until he was behind the driver's window. He rapped on it until it came down. "Banks, pull over. Now."

"Why does Martine think she's going to meet me?" Sydney repeated.

Chris held up his hand. "Can you please give me a minute? I need some air." As soon as the limo stopped moving, he was out the door and onto the sidewalk. He took a few steps and put his hands on his knees. Sydney stared out the window, watching his rib cage shrink and expand as he sucked in deep lungfuls of air. It was nearly a minute before he pulled out his cell phone.

Sydney looked at Benny, who suddenly became deeply interested in the lens cases in his camera bag. "Benny, what's going on?"

"I'm just the photographer," he said.

*

Chris' stomach turned over again. This wasn't a hangover flip or a hungry flip. This was a pretty-sure-I've-screwed-up-bad flip, and the fact he recognized it as such was worrisome. This was a screw-up of epic proportions if he was as right as he thought he was. After two years as a king of the Greek gods he was well versed in epic. So he did what he always did.

"Yo," the answering voice said.

"Nick, I think I'm in trouble," he started.

"She doesn't like cake?"

"I think I kidnapped somebody."

Dead air met his announcement. "What?"

"Sydney's in the limo. She thinks I'm dropping her off at her place, but we're on our way to the studio."

"Thank God. I thought you meant she was in the trunk." Nick laughed.

"I'm serious! I promised to take her home because she has plans for this afternoon, but I told Banks to drive us to the set. I was going to spring everything on her. I think she's going to be pissed."

"You think?" Sydney shouted behind him.

"Call you back," Chris said before he ended the call and slid the phone into his pocket. He held up his hands. "I can explain."

"I don't care." Sydney looked around until she spotted a street sign on the corner. "Oh my God! Do you have any idea how long it's going to take me to get home from here using public transit? You've blown my entire schedule to hell. Do you know how much it's going to cost me to take a cab? What the hell were you thinking?"

Perhaps it was another bad idea, but he went for the truth this time. "The studio was hoping that you would be willing to come to the set for a photo shoot. Pose for a few photographers, do a meet and greet with some of the cast. I told them you would." He hadn't finished getting the words out when he was struck with how arrogant his assumption was. It wasn't enough he was volunteering her for the afternoon when she'd flat out told him she had a prior commitment. He also was going to throw her unprepared into a situation that gave a lot of professional actors hives.

"I told you. I'm busy this afternoon. We had an agreement. You give me a ride; I give you my morning. Deal terminated."

"Would you please reconsider? It shouldn't be too long. They'll have lunch. You eat, don't you? I even called ahead and made sure they have cake. And I'll make sure you get to use the limo for the rest of the day. Banks will take you wherever you need to go. I promise."

This was not good. Her nice girl vibe vaporized as the full extent of his play hit her. He could see the stress radiating off her as she repeated herself. "First of all, your promises aren't holding much weight right now. Secondly, I didn't schedule a lunch break today because I don't have time for it."

"Please, this is important."

"As opposed to my plans, which aren't. Not that you've bothered to ask what they were."

Chris at least had the grace to blush. Sydney didn't look amused in the slightest. He didn't blame her. He knew this business. He knew firsthand what it was like to have yet another person assume they had the right to your time or attention or body with no respect to the fact it was your life they were invading. He could imagine exactly where she felt she stood. In her mind, it was under his heel.

"Sydney..."

"No. Let's see if I can have this conversation without

you, Chris. You have people who are expecting us to show up. You made a commitment, and you want to honor it. People are counting on your attendance because they've poured a lot of time and money into your event. How am I doing so far?"

"Pretty good."

"What a surprise. Guess what? I have people expecting me to show up. I want to keep my word about attending. I have invested time and money into my event. I may not be a movie star, but I am just as important as you are. So tell me, why do you expect me to make the sacrifice?"

He felt like a dick to hear it laid out like that. He didn't respond. He couldn't. He had no defense that didn't make him sound like the self-serving asshole he was. This karma thing was a bitch.

Chris walked back to the limo. He gripped the top of the open door and looked at Sydney sadly. He loved his life. He loved the attention and the adulation and the job he did to earn both. It sucked that he'd blown his shot at the High Note role. But he was surprised to feel the same amount of regret at having lost Sydney's respect. She'd done as she promised. She'd treated this morning like a blind date and him like a real person. Unlike him, she hadn't had an agenda. She just did her thing and had let him come along for the ride.

Karma could take him right now.

*

There were no words to describe her anger. Well, there were, but since Sydney suspected her mother had the ability to reach across three states with a bar of soap, she held her peace and bit her tongue. Hard.

Chris didn't let go of the limo door. He was going to dump her on the side of the road. Classy. At least they weren't in the boonies. She knew where she was and how to get home from here. It wouldn't be fun, but it was doable. It might be easier to call her best friend to come and get her. Sydney checked the street for a bus stop and saw one half a block up.

She walked around him and bent over to look into the backseat at Benny. "It was nice to meet you. Good luck with your photography career." The teenager stared at her, mouth moving but nothing coming out.

Then she turned and walked away.

"Where are you going? Why did you say good-bye to Benny?"

"To catch the bus since you're kicking me out of the limo."

"What makes you think I'm kicking you out of the limo?"

Sydney stopped in her tracks. "I'm out here, and the inside of the limo is in there, and you're in the way." She pointed at the blocked entrance to the idling vehicle.

"I'm not stopping you from getting back into the limo," Chris insisted. He looked down at his arm and how he was standing. "Okay, maybe I am, but I wasn't doing it on purpose. I have to tell you something, and I was working up the nerve."

"Tell me what?" There was nothing to discuss. He wanted something she wasn't prepared to give. Lines drawn, fight over. She won. Okay, Chris had won the battle by dropping her off twenty miles from her house, but she had won the war because, once she got home, the rest of the day was hers. This guy had made her think that actors were human, and in the end, he lived up to the stereotype of being a self-centered jerk who wanted to take advantage and use her to get ahead. Story of her freaking life.

"I'm sorry."

She was so confused. "For kicking me out of the limo?"

"I'm not kicking you out a million miles from your house."

"Twenty miles. Maybe fifteen."

"Can we stick to one subject at a time, please?"

"I don't know what the subject is!"

"Sydney, I am very sorry for assuming that my photo shoot this afternoon was more important than your plans. You're right; I didn't even ask what you were doing."

"Oh. Okay then."

"So, what are you doing?"

"I'm going to the beach."

Going by the insane tempo the vein on his forehead was beating at, Sydney thought his head was going to explode in the next three seconds. He started a breathing cycle of inhaling through his nose and exhaling through his mouth that she recognized as a relaxation technique. He wasn't good at it.

"You're blowing me off to go to the beach. Okay, I understand. That might be more important to you," Chris said slowly. "I can still drive you home at least. Thank you for this morning, especially since you didn't get any notice. I appreciate your time."

Chris swung his arm back to clear the doorway for her, but she grabbed it. She hadn't made the beach comment to be mean. She was simply too confused to be more clear. "Have you heard of the Curse the Darkness Foundation?" she asked.

"No."

"It's a small charity that helps burn victims. The idea behind it is that burn victims often stick to the shadows because of their scars. Curse the Darkness raises funds to help with plastic surgery so they aren't afraid to be seen in the light anymore." She bit her lip at the end of that extremely brief explanation.

There was so much more to her foundation than that, but this wasn't the time or place to discuss it with a guy she'd just met. She really didn't want to tell Chris she was one of those victims. The flirting would vanish and be replaced with sympathy so thick she'd choke on it. It always did.

A year ago she flirted as easily as breathing. She'd been doing it that night at Cosmo's. She remembered her waiter's name had been Carlos. She and the girls had gone out for her best friend's birthday, and all was right with the world. Until it exploded.

Sydney woke up pinned to the floor, caught under a table after a SUV crashed through the restaurant's front wall. Her view had been limited to the undercarriage and the fluids leaking out of it. At the time she thought she'd been lying next to a pool of gasoline, but it had actually been ouzo.

It didn't matter. They both burned. The ouzo just reached her first.

The rest was fuzzy. She'd seen the videos, the ones people had taken with their phones on the scene, and the ones the news crews had taken of the wreckage later. Sometimes she thought she had a real memory, but even now she was never quite sure. If she was being honest with herself, she didn't think she wanted to remember any more of that night.

"The foundation sounds like a good cause."

"It's a very good cause. It's a great charity, and its biggest fundraiser of the year starts at three o'clock this afternoon at Manhattan Beach. We're holding the final game for the thirty-two team beach volleyball league that has been raising money since Christmas."

"And you have to be there to organize?"

"I have to be there to play." Beach volleyball was one of the few things left in her life that she did for fun. She would have been playing without the fundraiser, but signing up for it cost her nothing but a little time finding sponsors. It also got her into another league, even if it was temporarily.

"Your team made it to the finals?"

"Of course we did. What kind of girl do you think I am? Anyway, I have to be there. Really, when I said this morning that any other weekend was preferable, I wasn't kidding. I need this afternoon and tonight. I'd help you if I could. Honestly. But this trumps meeting a roomful of people who want to take some goofy pictures of the two of us. I'm sorry."

"Don't apologize. You're right. That trumps a PR event any day." Chris took her arm and guided her back into the limo.

It was more important. It didn't mean she didn't want to go do a photo shoot with him at a real Hollywood soundstage. Sydney was rigidly scheduled, but she did know how to have fun and, honestly, the experience would have been cooler than hell. It didn't matter. She genuinely had someplace to be this afternoon, and she was not putting it off for a stranger who appeared on her doorstep, no matter how good he looked in khakis and a golf shirt that showed off his yummy tan.

The last fifteen miles were still silent, but the tension between them was gone. Benny fidgeted but refrained from speaking after Chris waved him off for the second time.

Her house appeared much too soon. Benny took a few more shots of Chris helping her out of the limo and escorting her to her door before disappearing back into the car.

"Thanks, Syd, for today. You have no idea what it meant to me."

She would have loved to lean in for a good-bye kiss—or a hug at the very least—but the whole situation was too awkward. She settled for a handshake and for a moment thought she saw the same regret in Chris' eyes. It would have been nice.

Sydney slid the key into the lock when she was spun around. Chris grabbed her by the arms and pulled her close, pressing a hard kiss to her mouth. She closed her eyes and stretched her hands out until they hit his chest. She leaned in to him and let go of the rest. His lips moved against hers, and Sydney swore the nerves in her lips were wired to the rest of her body. The sensation was indescribable. Then it was gone. Chris let her go and was down the steps before either of them had a chance to say a word.

Chapter 9

Sydney locked the row house door behind her and watched through the peephole as Chris retreated to the limo. She pulled her phone out of her purse and hit the first number on speed dial. Three rings later, the voice she most wanted to hear answered. "Hey, Syd, you ready to kick some booty?"

"Hey, Ashleigh," was all she had to say.

"What's wrong?"

It was relief beyond words to have a best friend who knew her so well and who could tell in two words everything she wasn't able to say.

"I just kicked a god to the curb."

"Which god are we talking about? A god? Or the God?" Ashleigh asked in clarification.

"You are such a Groundhog Day freak. A Greek god. Zeus."

"You know the rules. No dissing Mr. Murray. Also, Zeus? Chris 'Zeus' Peck? You won the Olympus sweepstakes and you didn't even mention it last night? I thought we were friends!"

"I didn't know last night." Sydney kicked off her shoes. One bounced off the television stand. The other landed on the piano bench in the corner and balanced precariously on the edge above the pedals. Sydney collapsed onto her loveseat with a groan. "He showed up at the butt crack of dawn this morning. Apparently I didn't receive my notification."

"Was he wearing his toga?" She'd forgotten that Ashleigh was a bigger fan than she was.

"He was wearing a tux."

A heavy sigh came across the line. "Call me back in fifteen minutes. I'll be in my bunk."

"Ash, this is serious. He wanted me to do a publicity thingy this afternoon."

"This afternoon? Can you reschedule?"

"No, it's part of the sweepstakes prize. They added it after the fact, thinking the winner would be more than pleased to go along with it. So not only did I not plan for Chris, I couldn't have planned for it."

The four word response was drawn out. "Oh, that just sucks."

That right there was exactly why Ashleigh Jessup was her first call. There was not a flicker of doubt in her friend's tone that Sydney had both turned down the photo shoot and that it was the right decision to make. "You can say that again. He just left."

"Tell me everything," Ashleigh insisted.

So she did, sparing no details about the tuxedo or the six-pack hugging golf shirt and khakis. Sydney had time to get a glass of water while Ashleigh recovered from her giggle fit when she heard about Polk and Odin. She held back the fact he'd held on to her hand a little longer each time he'd helped her into and out of the limo. And the kiss was her secret alone. That one thing she wanted to keep for herself. It wasn't sexy or flashy, but it was hers. Chris hadn't said anything, but it was enough to let her pretend there might have been something if they'd had a chance. It was more than she'd had for a while.

"And then he came up and met Nana."

There was silence on the line. "How did that go?"

"He thought I was a little rough on her when I raised my voice because she moved the fire extinguisher again."

"What did you do, Syd?"

"I may have told him to stick to show business and stay out of my family business." She couldn't help wincing as she remembered the look on his face when she'd snapped that at him. In any other instance, she would have loved the fact he was sticking up for her grandmother. He couldn't have known the old lady had been moved into an apartment without a stove for a reason.

"Harsh."

"I made it up to him by introducing him to the Dobsons. I think Mr. D is one of his heroes or something. Anyway, they hit it off. Then on the drive home, the show's PR person did a short interview with me over the phone—and remind me to get some screen captures of it on the site—and she said she looked forward to meeting me. At which point, Chris had the limo pull over and I overheard the part of his conversation where he was admitting that he wasn't taking me home like he'd promised but was kidnapping me to take me to the studio for the photo shoot. I yelled. He apologized and brought me home. The end."

The woman at the other end of the line snickered.

"Are you laughing at me, Ash?"

"Just a little. Only you could have something so good happen and have it go so very wrong."

Sydney threw herself on her living room sofa. "What time is it? Is it too early to start drinking?"

"How can you even think about booze after the sake last night?"

"Have you not been listening?"

Ashleigh gave her a moment to wallow in self-pity before hauling her back on track. "Are you still without a ride to the beach? I can swing by and pick you up around one," she offered.

"That would be great." The knocker on her front door echoed down the hallway. "Hold on a second. Someone's at my door."

"Are you expecting anyone?"

"No."

Sydney peeked through the peephole and nearly dropped the phone.

"Syd, who is it? Syd?" Ashleigh must have been yelling if she could hear her with the cell at her hip. She raised the phone to her mouth and whispered, "It's him."

"Him? Zeus?"

"Yeah, he's back. What do I do?"

"Open the damned door!"

* * * *

Chris made sure the driver waited until Sydney was inside her house before he drove away. This morning had alternated between divine and disaster like a rollercoaster. Karmically, though, he could see how it couldn't have ended any other way. Maybe his agent was right. This impulsive thing was kicking his ass. Rolling with it and seeing where he ended up was fun, but the price tag had officially become too high. Flushing the role and an afternoon with Sydney in the same move drove that home like nothing had before. The limo rounded the corner by Bella Bean when he decided he couldn't take it anymore.

"Banks, pull over."

Like any top chauffer in Los Angeles, the driver was able to find a space on the busy street within half a block. Benny didn't even look up. He was too busy downloading photos from Chris and Sydney's good-bye.

Chris jumped to the curb and paced in a tight circle for a full minute before he pulled out his phone. "Nicky, she's gone."

"Gone? You kidnapped her; then you lost her? What the hell are you doing? Go find her."

"She's not lost. She left."

"She can't do that."

"She can, and she did."

At the other end of the line, Nick whistled. "Not good, Chris. Martine and her lawyers are going to have a fit."

Nick wasn't kidding. The noise on the other end of the line quieted, and Chris heard a door close. "Where are you?"

"My trailer. She can't leave. It'll ruin everything," Nick whined.

Nick's denial of the situation was a pretty solid hint that he had been the one to set up the last minute photo shoot for this afternoon just to mess with him, and Nick was not taking the thought of changes to his prank well. He knew Chris was planning to use the sweepstakes as a lobby to get the rom-com role, but he wasn't above screwing with his best friend even while helping him out.

His co-star played Ares—the god of war—but he wasn't much for conflict. Nick Thurston was a golden boy in Hollywood, a child star born to two long-time, successful actors. He didn't do conflict because he always got what he wanted when he wanted it. Nick was the first to admit he was spoiled, but Chris was the first to say he wasn't an asshole about it. Chris had no idea how one guy could be so lucky. Nick seemed to be part Midas. He barely had to audition, if he did at all. As far as Chris knew, all of Nick's roles had been offered to him or created for him. Not to mention, every single project Nick got involved in was a success that never failed to turn a tremendous profit.

Chris didn't know how yet, but he knew Nick would find a way to turn this around and make it work for both of them. He kept pacing. There wasn't anything to lean against and no benches in sight. "She did. She never even received notification that I was coming over this morning."

"That's impossible."

Chris heard the crack of the seal on a water bottle breaking. "Want to bet? Guess who got the roses and my note? Russ," he said without waiting for an answer.

"That explains his mood this morning. When I got here, I thought he was going to kill me. It took forever to convince him I hadn't done whatever he thought I did."

"You're lucky he believed you at all." Chris understood the potency of his trainer's vengeance. Russ had fallen victim to one of Nick's pranks in the first season and had not been amused. Lesson learned—don't piss off the former navy guy in charge of your workouts.

"Who screwed that up?" Nick asked.

"My TV wifey's sister and oh-so-efficient assistant. Kristin didn't even speak to anyone. She left messages. If we didn't notify Sydney, we can't hold her responsible for not knowing."

"Then how'd you get her to agree to this morning?"

"My charm and good looks." The sad thing was that six hours ago, he would have believed it. After spending time with Sydney, he thought she might have seen something more to him. Until he'd blown it.

"Are you sure you explained it right? We are throwing this thing in her honor."

"She has a charity thing this afternoon. It's a really big deal to her. I can't ask her to blow it off because nobody from the show bothered to do a follow-up call. The show and the studio will look like assholes. Which also kills Martine's lawyer option."

"You're right, bro, you're screwed. The word is someone from High Note is going to be here."

Of course karma would give him that now.

There had to be a way. Had to. There must be

something he could do to get Sydney to agree to spend part of the afternoon with him without her missing her charity gig. He couldn't offer to write her a check; people expected her to show up to fundraise.

He was an idiot. Thank God he wasn't playing a genius.

"Nicky, I need a favor. A big one."

"Chris…"

"Nick, I have three words for you. Russ' birthday clown-o-gram."

Chris suffered through some unfiltered cursing before he heard the word he wanted. "What?"

"We, meaning you, me and whoever else we can grab, are all going down to Manhattan Beach to root for Sydney's beach volleyball team and be a presence for her charity this afternoon."

"Dude, you know I'd do anything for you, but this doesn't help with the photo shoot."

"I'm going to talk to her. She'll agree." He might have to beg, but she'd agree in the end. Chris could smooth things over with the PR department. They'd put this thing together at the last minute. It wasn't like the schedule was set in stone. He'd explain the afternoon didn't have to be one-sided. They could get her to the studio, run her through hair and makeup, do the deed so to speak, and then all of them drive out to the beach for some more press ops. It was perfect. As long as she said yes.

"Call me back when she says yes." Nick hung up without saying good-bye.

Now he was stuck. Did he get back into the limo and have Banks circle around and try to linger on a busy residential street? He could run there in the time it took for the limo to make the first turn. That was the answer.

He tapped on the passenger side window until the chauffer opened it. "Stay here," he instructed. "I'll be back in a couple minutes."

Dodging pedestrians as he ran back to Sydney's house reminded him of the endings to half a dozen movies he'd seen over the years. Of course, this was nothing like a romantic comedy, starting with the fact if this sprinting thing worked, it wouldn't be the end of the story. The people on the sidewalk weren't cheering him on. It wasn't raining.

Oh, and the fact Sydney wasn't his girl. If it worked, she would be for a while longer, but it wouldn't be his happily-ever-after. If he were really lucky, it would be her forgiving him and tolerating him for the rest of the afternoon, only without the easy, friendly, flirting vibe they'd established earlier. He'd prefer another kiss, but he'd settle for civil if he could get it.

There were her flower boxes and her front steps. And there was her door.

He had nothing left to lose.

Chapter 10

Sydney opened the door. Chris was leaning on the guardrail to the steps. He raised his head and waved a hand.

"Um, hi?" She sounded like a moron.

"Hey."

Damn, hot and sweaty and breathing hard was attractive. She stepped out and checked the curb. The limo wasn't in sight. "Where did you come from?"

Chris pointed down the street.

That was a completely accurate yet unhelpful answer. "Would you like to come in?"

Sydney got him a bottled water from the fridge while he inspected the posters lining her hallway as he made his way toward the kitchen. He stopped in front of the Ghostbusters one. "I love this movie," he told her. "Where did you get this?"

"Present, present, eBay," she said as she pointed to various frames. "I grew up with these films. I love them."

He accepted the water with a nod and proceeded to empty half the bottle. "Aren't you a little young to be a child of the eighties?"

She didn't try to hold back the slow smile that spread across her face as she admired her prized artwork. She'd watched them a hundred times over last year. Those films were her safe place and never failed to bring her mood up. They'd done it when she was little, and now that she was older, she appreciated the subtext and humor she'd missed in her youth. "My parents are huge movie buffs. When I was a kid, if they came on television, we watched. Then we watched them on VHS, then DVD. When they came out on Blu-ray, my parents bought three copies and mailed one to me and one to my brother. I swear I know them all by heart."

Chris dropped his voice and leaned in like he was telling her a secret. "My mom is a huge John Hughes fan. I can quote every single Molly Ringwald line. Don't judge."

That was too adorable. She could quote them too, but she wasn't going to admit it now. Sydney led him into the living room and picked up her water glass. She settled into the loveseat and pretended she wasn't about to come out of her skin from sheer nerves. "Not that I didn't have fun this morning, because I did, but why are you back here? I thought our good-bye was pretty definite. And where is young Benny to record the moment?"

"Tell me more about the Curse the Darkness fundraiser, Sydney." He nudged her shoe onto the floor and leaned back onto the piano's water-stained keyboard cover.

She'd expected a flood of over-the-top apologies. Possibly threats of a lawsuit for violating the contest's increasingly irritating terms of service agreement. Not what appeared to be genuine interest in her life. "This afternoon is the volleyball tournament with a silent auction on the sidelines. We've been hitting up personal and corporate sponsors since Christmas. There were originally thirty-two two-person teams. Two weeks ago, we started the playoffs with the top eight. This afternoon is the finals: Team Scar versus Team Veggie Delight." Sydney didn't have a clue why he wanted to know.

"Which team are you on?"

"My friend Ashleigh and I are Team Scar. We know a lot of guys in the burn unit at the local VA hospital."

"Good. I don't know if I could have supported you with a name like Team Veggie Delight."

"It is rather lame," she agreed. Wait a minute.

"Supported me?"

"I thought I could come down and cheer you on. Maybe raise a little interest for you by putting something on one of the show's online accounts? You haven't said anything, but I am a little famous." He mock-blushed at the last line. It would have been cute if it weren't a shameless bribe.

"I can't help you, Chris. It sounds like a riot, but I can't."

"I'd love for you to come to the set. But either way I'll show up at your tournament. When do you have to be there?"

"The game starts at three thirty. I have to be in my gear and at the court at quarter to three at the very latest to sell tickets and help prep."

"It's only eleven now. We could have you on the set by noon and be done by two. If you want to come."

"This isn't about me winning the sweepstakes. The show wouldn't care that much. Why do you want me there so bad?" Sydney was fishing. She didn't know there was something else, but it was a fair assumption. Events fell apart all the time, and the show's PR people had more than enough to fake it. This was something else.

Chris' jaw dropped. Ding, ding, ding. Even actors needed a second to get their reactions under control when slapped in the face with the unexpected truth. She'd nailed it on the head. Sydney didn't know what it was, but it was big. At least to Chris.

"The show doesn't," he agreed slowly.

"But…"

"But I care." He stopped there and stared at her.

She smiled back. Not a "fine, I'll give you a pass" smile either. A "get busy explaining" one.

"Do you know the name High Note?"

For once, Sydney sat on her smart ass remark before it got out of her mouth and shook her head instead. The man in front of her was too…what was the word? Serious, perhaps. Earnest. Whatever it was, it was a side of him she hadn't seen before. It wasn't like he could kidnap her out of her house, so she felt she could give him a minute.

"They're a movie production company. They're casting a romantic comedy right now, and there's a role I want very badly. This 'slave for a day' gig was supposed to be a pre-audition for me. Very public and very risky. I pretty much bet the role on this sweepstakes. Even before the winner was announced, I did everything but offer money to get one of the movie's producers to meet us at the set."

"You don't do rom-coms." Ashleigh's voice piped through the cell phone's tiny speaker.

Sydney snatched up her phone from the coffee table. "Oh my God, Ash, are you still there?"

"You put me on speaker when you dropped me in your run to the door," her friend said.

Chris leaned in. "Who is this?"

"I'm Ashleigh Jessup, Syd's best friend, volleyball partner, and partner in crime."

Jesus. "Ashleigh!"

"What? It's not like he's a cop."

Chris' eyebrow shot up. "Is there something I should know?"

"No." The answer hit him in stereo, but Sydney meant hers, and Ash made hers sound like a question.

"So if Sydney doesn't show up, you won't get the part?" Ashleigh clarified.

"Yes. Kind of. If she doesn't show up, I won't get it. If she does show up, I still might not get it," he elaborated.

"Syd, you should do this. I'll handle the setup part. Have some fun for once."

"I have fun," Sydney protested. The tournament was going to be fun. Flirting with Chris this morning had been fun. Last night had been fun. Until the sake.

"Tell me again why you're not working tomorrow?" Ashleigh pushed.

"Not appropriate, Ash."

"Why isn't she working tomorrow, Ash?" Chris asked.

"Because somebody burned through all her overtime. For the quarter. By the end of January. Although I have no idea why she'd want to pick up any shifts."

"It pays well."

"Lame, Sydney. Chris Peck, do you absolutely swear that you can have her on the court and ready to go by quarter to three?"

Sydney took the phone off speaker and held it to her ear. "What are you doing?" she whispered as she headed into the hall. Sydney was used to being the practical one when it came to her group of friends, but this was ridiculous. Ash had officially lost her mind if she thought Sydney was going to skip out on the afternoon's activities.

"Do this."

"Excuse me, Ash, but we have plans. I know this because I'm the one who made them."

Ashleigh sighed heavily over the phone. "You are never going to get this chance again."

"I know." It sucked, but it was true.

"There are a dozen other people who are going to be working prep for the tournament. You trained us well, sensei. Besides, you have your phone. Go. Do this. Just get your ass to the beach on time. We can handle it."

"I promised—" Sydney started.

"Sydney, do this." Her friend's tone brooked no argument, and Ashleigh was seldom serious. It went against her nature. "We all know what you've done, and what you are willing to do. You deserve this. The timing stinks, but we can't do anything about it. We can cover for you. Forget about your schedule and your to-do lists and for once just run with it. Trust me. You need to do this."

Sydney didn't have a response to that. The idea of leaving the playoff organization in somebody else's hands was too big for her brain.

"Ash?"

"Put me back on speaker."

Sydney did.

"Hey. Manhattan Beach. Two forty-five this afternoon. Do you swear?" Ashleigh repeated.

Chris looked at Sydney more seriously than she'd ever seen him. "I swear. If you talk her into this, Ashleigh, I won't know how to thank you."

"Just make sure you get her there on time, and maybe you could bring a couple of your friends with you? I'll see what I can do about finding some last minute donation forms. Because you will be bringing your checkbook, right?"

"Absolutely. I'll make sure the show puts something together for your auction as well." Chris looked at her, waiting. Her reasons for refusing started to fade until she was left with no excuses. Ashleigh had taken them all away. She'd already admitted she wanted to do it. She'd never have another chance to get onto an honest-to-Greek-god television set. The only thing holding her back was her promise to finish off the volleyball tournament. If she could do both, it could be the best day she'd had in recent memory. Possibly all memory.

"Okay," Sydney agreed. "Per your negotiated conditions with Ashleigh, I'm in."

"Syd, take me off speaker again."

She did. "What?"

"Kiss on it," Ashleigh suggested with a giggle.

"What?"

"You may never get another chance to kiss Zeus. I'm helping."

"You've already helped enough, thank you very much. Besides, that is against the sweepstakes' terms of service agreement."

The phone was out of her hand before she had time to react. She managed to spit out a "hey".

Chris dodged around to the far side of the coffee table. "What exactly did you suggest she do that violated the terms of service, Ashleigh?" He listened for a moment. "Okay." He listened for a while longer and gave her friend other words of agreement. "Okay, bye." He ended the call and handed the phone back to her. "Can you be ready to go in fifteen minutes?"

"I can be ready in five. Let me touch up my makeup."

"Don't worry, we'll have our hair and makeup people waiting. Not that you need it," he added. He stared at her like she had something in her teeth.

"What?" she asked.

"I'm a little stunned that you could be ready in five minutes."

Now that she had the rest of the afternoon to flirt, she wasn't going to waste it. "Do you have a stopwatch?"

Chris pointed to the watch on his left wrist. "Yes." He dropped his hand back to his side and looked at her again.

"What?" Sydney repeated.

He leaned forward and brushed his lips over hers. It was nothing like the kiss they'd shared on the front steps. This one was soft and warm. It was a hint of what could come. If the quickie at the door hadn't already set her knees to knocking, this more than made up for it. He wasn't even touching her anywhere else.

"To seal the deal," Chris said.

Sweet mother of pearl. She shivered as his low voice caused her entire body to tense up. If he'd used tongue she'd be a puddle on the floor by now.

"What about the terms of service?" she asked breathlessly.

"I think we can agree they've pretty much crashed and burned at this point. Don't you?"

Sydney nodded.

He stepped back and pressed a button on his watch so it beeped. "Go."

She ran.

Chapter 11

He had to be the luckiest son of a bitch on the planet. It was entirely possible he had a guardian angel named Ashleigh. Of course, if he missed getting Sydney to the beach, his angel had threatened to remove parts of him he might want to use with Sydney at a later date, and she'd sounded deadly serious about doing it. He wasn't going to take the chance. In order to avoid that fate, all he had to do was move up a publicity event, get in and out without anything going wrong, and coerce some castmates who had no idea they'd been volunteered for a charity event. No problem. They were going to kill him, but it wouldn't be until after his day with Sydney. It might even end up being worth it.

Why did he have to meet her today? Sure, some actors met regular people, but it was hard to find someone outside the industry who understood the craziness of it. Sydney did. He'd risked it all when he told Sydney the whole truth about today, and she got it. No, it was more than that. He'd messed up, he apologized, and she'd still given him a chance to explain. She didn't launch into histrionics or go screaming to the nearest media outlet about what an asshole he'd been. She'd handled it and him. Nobody wanted to handle him. Even his agent passed him off to a life coach as a last resort. Sydney called him on his bullshit, and he made the decision to man up because he wanted to make good for her. It was selfish as hell, but he wanted someone like that in his life.

Not to mention, they had chemistry like he'd never experienced. It took everything he had not to ask her out for real after that kiss and do it again. But if Sydney had shivered and he'd needed to adjust his belt after barely a peck on the lips, a good one might bring the need for the fire extinguisher in the hall. Finding chemistry with a woman in his professional world would be like striking gold. Actors prayed for sizzle like that in front of the camera. The romantic comedy audition would be in the bag if he and his co-star reacted half that well.

He was supposed to be doing something. Right, the studio. He scrolled through his contacts but stopped. This was Nicky's fault; he should deal with the PR people. They loved him anyway. Chris hit speed dial.

"Chris, did you get her?"

"I sealed the deal. Did you order the cake?"

"It's on the way," Nick promised.

"I need another favor."

"In addition to the charity gig afterward?"

"Yes."

"You're pushing your luck, Chris. What do you need now?"

"I need you to move up your little surprise party to noon and absolutely guarantee we are all in the limo and on the way to Manhattan Beach by two o'clock."

"Dude, do you know how impossible that is? Martine is going to scream."

"It's the only way. Grab her fast and tell her about the free publicity for helping out our winner's charity. Hell, tell Layla how badly her sister screwed up and make her toss in her support if she wants Kristin to keep her job. Russ will verify the bad calls. With all three of us, Martine won't have a choice. She won't be happy, but she'll do it. Then I'll give her a call."

"You are screwing me big-time on this, Chris," Nick complained.

"You set this up without telling me, buddy. That's the problem with surprise parties. Sometimes the recipient isn't the only one who is surprised."

"Yeah, this didn't quite work out as planned. But we'll be even after this, right?"

"Absolutely." The threat of telling Layla that Nick was the one to have her car towed off the set last week after she'd parked in Nick's labelled personal spot for the third day running threat was only good for so long anyway, and it was starting to lose its potency. Besides, it was Nick. There would always be more ammunition.

"You don't ask for much. Fine, press phalanx at noon, with cake, followed by a quick escape at two o'clock and an afternoon of fundraising on the beach, even though it's St. Valentine's weekend and some of us have dates."

"Quit reading Bridget Jones."

"Dude, you recognized the quote."

"I have two sisters. You don't."

"I can appreciate women's literature."

"You appreciate Renee Z. Get to work." The End Call button was a wonderful thing.

This might actually work. Shit. He forgot to ask Chris if the High Note people were on the lot yet. Sydney was thawing toward him; he could tell. She'd forgiven him for the near kidnapping. He needed the movie producers to see he could be cast as an average guy who could catch a regular girl. Sydney might have to turn it down a notch to pass for average though. Nobody would believe that someone outside the business could fake calm and charm industry pros like she had. He wasn't certain how she was doing it, but she had definitely pulled it off with Mr. Dobson, and him. Maybe it had something to do with her job. He could see that working in a call center would definitely gain her some skills in swinging people's opinions her way.

Maybe he could ask her not to...Karma, stupid. If he could have smacked himself in the back of the head without attracting attention to himself, he would have. He would not ask Sydney to be less than she was to make him look better. Karma was putting others first, not belittling them. Besides, if she impressed him, she'd impress the studio people. Showing up with an extraordinary woman like her would be an even better coup. He got lucky with his owner for the day, and everyone was going to know it.

Not that he had the role in the bag yet. He got Martine on the line and gave her more details than he'd given Nick. They were right. She screamed. Fortunately, very little of it was at him. With any luck, Layla would have been on the receiving end about her sister's screw-up, and Nick would have gotten it about his unplanned event, and the worst of the fireworks would be over by the time they arrived. Chris had cautioned her that absolutely nothing was to blow back on their grand prize winner.

He turned around and jumped when Sydney arrived in the doorway. She'd changed into a pretty blue and white striped sundress and strappy white sandals. It reminded him of the dress his sister had worn to his parents' thirtieth anniversary party. It had that "I'm expensive" sheen and stiffness to the material. It also covered a very respectable amount of skin. He'd now seen Sydney in three different outfits and still hadn't gotten a good glimpse of cleavage. Chris was starting to think it was a conspiracy. "Are you ready to go?" she asked.

"Are you?"

She hefted a backpack. "All I need is a place to change."

"I'm going to have to get back into my tux if I want to keep up with you."

"What?"

"You look very nice." He tugged at his belt.

"Should we get going?"

"Yes, absolutely." He took her bag on the way out, and waited on the front step while she locked the door behind them. She looked out onto the street and hesitated when the limo was not parked up the street like it had been earlier that morning.

"Dude, where's your car?" Sydney asked with a laugh.

"I left it up past the coffee shop."

"So how did you get here?"

Saying he ran sounded a little too desperate. "I needed some time to think up my master plan."

"Bribery is your master plan?"

"It worked, didn't it?"

"Just so you know, I would have done it for free on any other day." She looked so earnest. He believed her. He could absolutely see her agreeing to spend the day with a stranger to help him out, and making sure they had a good time doing it. She was doing a great job as it was. The least he could do was return the favor.

"I know. That's why I'm going to help out your fundraiser. You deserve it."

"Thanks again for that." She stared at him for a minute. "Chris, the limo?"

"Right." Fortunately, he had the driver's number. They stood on the sidewalk gathering a fair share of looks and people taking pictures on their phones before the limo pulled up.

Benny threw the door open and hopped out as soon as it stopped moving. He whistled at Sydney, who blushed outrageously at the compliment. She stood beside Chris as Benny snapped away, and let him help her into the limo yet again. Chris couldn't be certain, but he thought the kid's zoom lens was getting a workout, and it hadn't been pointed in his direction.

"I'm going to have to hit wardrobe, aren't I?" Chris asked him as he tucked Sydney's bag against the back of the driver's seat.

"Not at all."

"I think I'd better." Chris sent a text directly to Martine asking she have navy slacks and a white button-down shirt waiting for them when he arrived. Adding "Nick will explain everything" crossed the line a bit, but considering she hadn't cleared the event beforehand with him either, he was certain he'd be given some slack since he'd come through for her.

"I think you're going to need your running shoes this afternoon, Benny," Sydney teased.

"We just have the sweepstakes party, don't we?" the photographer asked.

"Nope. Chris is my slave for the whole day. After that we are going to the beach." She turned to look at him as he sat beside her. "I'm thinking pompoms would be appropriate."

"I'm bringing Nick Thurston and God-knows-who-else to your fundraiser."

"Good, they can have pompoms too. Do you want to practice your cheer now?"

Benny was in hysterics. And, damn it, Chris knew he was going to end up shaking his pompoms. "I thought you believed in karma," Chris whined.

"Karma will get a kick out of it. I promised you no humiliation, but a little embarrassment will keep you humble."

Sydney got tense beside him as they entered the studio lot. Really tense of the stop talking, barely breathing kind. He reached over and grabbed one of her hands that she had clenched around her skirt.

"Hey, Syd, what's up?"

"Nothing."

"Would it help if I told you there was going to be cake?"

"You can't have cake."

"No, but you can."

"You got me cake?" Her face lit up, and her fist loosened enough that he was able to slide the material out of it and thread his fingers through hers.

"Absolutely, unless Nick fell down on the job."

"Can he eat cake?"

"Yes."

"I'll bet he got it then. Most men won't pass up cake." Sydney gave him a look that radiated pity. She was right too. Nick probably got a vanilla layer cake with chocolate icing just because it was Chris' favorite and Nick knew he couldn't have any. Bastard.

"Are you ready to be the guest of honor?"

"Have I mentioned how much I really don't like being photographed?"

Chris looked over at the photographer. "Benny, can you give us a couple minutes, please?"

Benny hopped out the door, and Chris watched through the window as he crossed over to Martine, who was waiting outside, and started showing her the latest batch of photos on the camera's screen.

Chris squeezed her hand. "These are all good people. My castmates are great. And Martine Peeples, the blonde outside, knows you are helping us out. She'll keep everything under control. I promise." She'd better. For all the screaming she'd done when Nick had originally told her that the sweepstakes winner may not be able to attend, she had better make it worth Sydney's time, especially considering the serious phobia his "master" had when it came to cameras. He'd checked some of the pictures Benny had posted. Sydney looked like cornered prey when she had to pose. The candid shots of her were practically of a different person as she radiated smiles and laughter. They looked good together, to the point where several of the spectators had noted the fact.

The limo door opened from the outside. Chris saw a row of people waiting for them, including Martine, Benny, and Robert Clancy. Robert "the Moneyman" Clancy. If Chris thought Nick had a near golden touch when it came to picking projects, Robert Clancy was Midas unleashed. Chris had hoped a senior producer would show but hadn't dreamed of the senior executive man of the project.

All of a sudden he was glad it was Sydney sitting beside him. They were waiting for him. This was it. All he needed was a couple minutes to set the stage. He pressed Sydney's hand into the seat. "Would you prefer to wait in here or explore for a couple minutes?"

"You're not leaving me alone with those people, are you?"

"I need to get changed."

"Why? You look fine."

"I've got to keep up with you, gorgeous." God, she was cute when she blushed. His family would have a heyday teasing her. He was learning she gave as good as she got, but it didn't stop the blushing. They'd love her. "You'd show me up horribly if we went out on the town tonight."

"I'm busy tonight. It's the gala evening to wrap up

fundraising," she said quickly. "Not that you were asking me out or anything."

If this karma thing were real, maybe if he kept treating her right, she'd continue to reward him for it. "The day is still young."

She stared at him, like she couldn't believe he was serious. He barely believed it himself, but he thought he meant it. He had to get out of the limo before he forgot while they were both there. "I'll be right back."

He needed five to ten minutes to change, even though the fantastic Mr. Banks had stopped fifty feet from his trailer, and at least another five to schmooze with Clancy before he escorted Sydney to the set for her debut in her role of "proof Chris Peck could be a leading everyday guy". He trusted his coworkers to do right by her. She'd do fine.

Chapter 12

I can do this. I can do this. Sydney thought she was speaking under her breath, but Chris' sideways look told her otherwise. She pressed her lips together and continued the mantra in her head. I can do this. Then she realized it wasn't optional. She could and would do this. It was exactly the same thing she'd be doing later, with fewer pictures and more strangers. This could be a practice run that wouldn't cost her donations if she screwed up. This disaster of Chris' making was a good thing. Sydney lifted her chin and forced her panicked grimace to morph into a genuine smile. She'd meet some people, shake some hands, maybe loosen some checkbooks. Just like she would tonight. No problem at all.

Speaking of hands, Chris was holding hers again as he pulled her out of the back of the limo. She stepped toward the woman in the dress even as Chris was finishing the introductions.

"Martine, this is Sydney Richardson, our Olympus grand prize winner who, despite having no notice at all about today's events, has generously agreed to help us out. Syd, this is Martine Peeples, our public relations spokesperson—she has events like this down to an art, and is well aware of your timetable."

Sydney gave her a real handshake, not a wimpy finger squeeze, and the woman smiled. Then Sydney turned to the gentleman in the suit. "Are you one of the show's producers?"

It seemed logical, but when Chris almost swallowed his tongue, she realized she'd guessed wrong. This was one of the movie guys he was trying to impress. Before Chris had a chance to correct her, she forged ahead on her own. "Hello, I'm Sydney Richardson."

The gray-haired man in the black suit smiled. "I'm Robert Clancy. I am a producer but not one for the show. Can I steal Chris away for a minute or two?"

Chris and the producer veered away to the trailers lined up beside the soundstage. Martine took her arm and steered her toward the soundstage. "Did Chris tell you what was going to happen?" the woman asked.

Sydney nodded. "I'm getting my hair and makeup done, and then we're meeting a couple of actors in the cast and taking some pictures." That Greek god of hers had five minutes to reappear and rescue her or she was going to hunt him down like a dog.

It turned out Martine was a genuinely nice, genuinely blonde California girl who went slightly overboard with the compliments as a thank you to Sydney for going along with the last minute schedule change. The poor woman had been frantic as she explained the notification mix-up. Sydney was trying to brush off the promised arrangements of flowers in apology when they arrived at a trailer marked "Hair/Makeup".

Whether she got here accidentally or not, Sydney had to admit that being on a studio lot was freaking cool. The trailer had head shots of all the Olympus stars and their assorted hairstyles. She recognized all the main actors and actresses, and she was stunned by the transformations in the photos. They became gods and goddesses in the very same chair she was sitting in.

It only took a couple minutes to realize the real goddesses were the women who worked in the trailer. The makeup artist made her eyes look amazing, lips lush, and skin glow. Sydney outright giggled when the hair stylist went into raptures at her natural red hair. She ended up undoing the French braid and letting the waves fall loosely around Sydney's shoulders, using only a handful of strategically placed bobby pins to style it. Hollywood magic was real and, damn, it made her look good.

"Now we have another surprise for you," Martine announced with a smile as Sydney met her at the bottom of the trailer steps.

Sydney looked around, but her slave for the day was nowhere in sight. "Where's Chris?" Getting made up like a glamour puss was one thing, but he promised she wouldn't be on her own for the photo shoot and studio tour. She could do it on her own. She just didn't want to. She liked Chris being around. Besides, this whole thing was so the two of them could appear together. Her doing it alone was kind of pointless.

A handful of hard-bodied men and women in togas ran into the sound studio. Sydney pressed herself against the trailer to get out of their way. Hollywood was full of the unexpected.

"He's getting changed in his trailer. Why don't we wait for him over at wardrobe?" Martine suggested.

"That's okay," Sydney replied in a helpful tone. "We can pick him up on the way."

Martine looked ready to protest.

"I insist," Sydney continued. "After all, he's the reason I'm here for the next ninety minutes." She walked to the end of the trailer. "Which way is it?" Three years of working in the complaints department of a hospital's call center taught her plenty of ways to change the direction of the conversation. She usually shifted it from getting screamed at to empathizing with the caller before getting down to the technical details of the call. At least today, the PR woman couldn't yell.

When Martine pointed left, Sydney smiled in thanks.

"I've been afraid to look at your sweepstakes page. How does it look with Benny's pictures? I know I don't photograph very well. He's been snapping away like crazy." Now that she was walking, she could see the actors' names on the doors. Chris' was next.

"The pictures are fine," Martine assured her. "Benny has some good candid ones of the two of you. I love the ones with Chris walking the cat."

"Odin is very photogenic," Sydney agreed with a snicker. "I thought Chris was going to have a conniption fit when he saw Polk and I offered him the pooper scooper."

Martine's eyes got wide. Then she turned to Benny, who had appeared out of nowhere and was walking beside them. "He what? Tell me you got that shot!"

Benny smirked. "Of course. It might have gotten buried in the comments though. People are going nuts on the sweepstakes page. We've had hundreds of Likes and retweets. That's why I was coming to find you. They're waiting for new ones. So what's the game plan?"

That's what Sydney wanted to know. She checked her watch. If she gave herself forty-five minutes to get from the studio to Manhattan Beach, assuming she changed here, she'd have to leave at two. Forty-five minutes was a conservative drive-time that gave her a slight window if she needed it. That left eighty-two minutes for Chris' part of the deal. She went so far as to set the alarm on her wristwatch. They needed to get this photo shoot in gear. "Why don't we ask Chris?" Sydney knocked on the trailer door with the "Zeus" sign.

It opened immediately. But not by Chris. Nick Thurston—the god of war—was resplendent in a blinding white toga and golden laurels in his highlighted hair. He looked so good that Sydney forgot why she was knocking on the door. Right behind him was a hulking toga-clad man with auburn hair down to his shoulders. Eros, aka Sean Glenn. Part of her thought Chris had been messing with her when he said she'd be meeting some of his co-stars. She'd made a big enough fool out of herself when she'd met Chris. The taste of shoe leather was barely out of her mouth. Now this? Meeting the whole cast would turn her into a drooling mess.

"Sydney, it's nice to meet you," Nick said.

When he spoke her name, she was pretty sure her mouth started watering. She nodded hello to them. The make the talk thing with the speaking things was not good. Words, that's what they were called. She forgot them all. So she nodded again.

"Chris is almost done. He'll be right out."

She was as stiff as a board when they stood beside her for a couple pictures. Yeah, Chris was a big television star, but he was a person. Nick was a movie star with movie star parents, and Sean had been a college basketball all-star at her parents' alma mater before he went into show business. A girl could only handle so many gods at once.

When the king of Olympus did arrive, Sydney touched her lips to make sure she wasn't drooling. Chris had eschewed the classic Greek look and went with contemporary upper crust. His shirt cost more than her dress. She could cut herself on the creases of his pants. And Sydney was certain his loafers would pay her rent for at least two months. She wasn't going to break her brain calculating the value of his cufflinks or watch. The sparkles coming from them indicated more carats than she had in her refrigerator crisper.

Then she remembered she looked damn good too. Her dress wasn't designer, but it was very nice. Her hair and makeup were almost good enough to make her look like she belonged.

Chris evidently thought so. He mock-grabbed her from Nick, mugging for the camera. He dipped her and growled at his co-star like a possessive beast. Sydney laughed. She loved it. His hand supported her at her waist and slid up. He hesitated when he got to her bra strap. She didn't mean to, but she couldn't help but stiffen when his fingers trailed the edge of her scars.

Behind her, Martine coughed once. Sydney twisted her neck and saw her shaking her head at Chris. Sydney looked back at him and felt her heart drop at the scowl he was wearing. Chris pulled his hand away and stood her back up.

"Sorry," he whispered in her ear. "Are you all right?"

"Fine." She knew exactly why he stopped at her shoulder. At least she'd missed whatever his initial reaction had been before he morphed it into a frown.

The others burst out laughing when Chris threatened his television son with a well-placed thunder bolt. Then his attention, but not his hand, was back on her. "Why are you still in your dress?" he asked.

"What?" Cost be damned, Sydney caught him by the front of the shirt and pulled him down until his ear was at her mouth. "Terms of service," she whispered.

He laughed. "No, no, no!" He laughed in an echo of their conversation this morning. He looked at Benny, and another photographer who had joined the group, and explained, "They're waiting to do a quick fitting over in wardrobe. You're getting the whole Olympus experience."

"What?"

"You get to have your own toga!" he said with a grin.

Sydney froze. "No thank you," she declined firmly. It was a lot more polite than the "No way in hell!" she wanted to scream.

Chris grabbed her wrist. "Come on, it'll be fun to go Greek."

She yanked her hand out of his grasp. "No. I don't wear things like that. Ever." Sydney took two steps back and stared him down. She recognized how shrill she sounded, but she didn't care.

"You've worn more revealing things than that before," a feminine, lyrical voice said from behind Chris. A small woman with a thick black braid of hair that fell to her waist linked her arm through Chris'.

"Sydney, I'd like to present—"

"We've met," Sydney interrupted.

Of all the film lots in all of Los Angeles, Layla Andrews had to walk onto this one while Sydney was there. They'd met a few times actually. Most recently it had been when Sydney had given her victim impact statement at Layla's sentencing after the woman had put Sydney in the hospital. The actress had gotten off with probation and a seal on the case prohibiting anyone from discussing the details of it. Like the fact Layla had been intoxicated at the accident scene.

"I didn't think you'd volunteer for this," Sydney commented through gritted teeth.

"I didn't." Layla's polite response was even more forced than Sydney's comment. Good. Make her squirm. The actress who played Hera, Zeus' wife, continued, "I'm required to do a number of public relations events, and this is one of them. Believe me, I'd rather be working the golf tournament next month."

"Believe you?" The woman could claim to be on fire and Sydney would ask for verification from two independent sources. Layla's story had changed every time she'd given a statement.

Layla turned her back to her and spoke directly to Chris and Martine. "I'll meet you inside. I hope this doesn't take too long."

"That makes two of us," Sydney muttered.

Chris and Martine had a whispered conversation while Sydney studied the tops of her sandals and waited for the embarrassed flush to cool from her cheeks. Even the sight of that woman put her blood pressure through the roof. There was no way she'd be able to get through the rest of this circus.

Chris held up his hands. "Martine's going to talk to wardrobe, so no worries." His eyes belied his words, but he kept his smile firmly fixed in place. "How about a tour of the set?"

Sydney tried to smile, although her face felt like it might crack a bit. "That sounds really cool."

He held out his hand again, and this time she took it.

"Awesome! Let's get this party started!"

Chapter 13

Robert Clancy liked him. For the role, liked him. The super-producer hadn't said so in so many words, but he'd complimented him on his day with Sydney so far and told Chris that the photos of the two of them showed the type of attitude his leading man would need. It was practically a yes. All Chris needed to do now was show him a little more to push him over the edge.

Nick told him it had taken some doing, some bribing, and some threatening, but Layla was on set. In fact, he said the actress had pitched a fit of epic proportions when Martine had volunteered her to make the trip to the beach with Sydney. Apparently contract appearance clauses had been invoked. Chris wasn't sorry he'd missed it. His TV wife's everyday drama was hard enough to stomach; he didn't want to deal with it off-set as well.

The fourth cast member who'd be tagging along on their field trip was Eros, which was a great choice. Sean Glenn played the god of love and attracted women as it if were true. The towering redhead's Monday morning play-by-play of the weekend starlets he'd bedded were legendary among the male cast and crew. So long as he kept his distance from Sydney, Chris was happy to have him along. He'd bring in a shitload of cash.

Martine had also managed to scrounge up the actors that played Aphrodite, Apollo, and Artemis for pictures. They'd be in costume, even if the guest of honor wouldn't be. Chris had no idea what was going on with Sydney and the toga. He thought it had been a great idea, although he'd been shocked to hear how it came about. Something must have happened between Martine's announcement and their arrival on set because Layla's-sister-slash-his-inept-assistant had told him Layla was the one who'd arranged the surprise. He wanted to ask Sydney what the deal was, but he didn't want to offend her after witnessing her reaction to the proposal. Maybe the fact he hadn't seen any cleavage wasn't karma working against him. Maybe she was modest.

He didn't have time to figure it out now. It was picture time. They arranged themselves in Zeus' great hall because it was the most impressive set they had that wasn't hot. The thrones and banquet table were all decked out, and the actors cracked wise as they hung out and posed for the cameras. They were having a great time, but Sydney looked like someone had shoved a stick up her ass. She wasn't relaxing or enjoying the shoot at all. She was trying hard, chatting everyone up and following the instructions of Benny and the other photographer. Something was very wrong with her. And she was killing his chances with the real kingmaker who was watching from the wings.

Benny had insisted the first few photos be of just the two of them. Then Chris called his castmates over and let them have their time with the lady of the hour. She flashed him a couple puzzled looks as he gradually got bumped farther and farther down the line from her but never said a word.

The intern was in heaven. Benny ordered the stars around and called shots like he knew what he was doing. They took it good-naturedly, and Sydney didn't know any differently. Right up to the point when Sean and Nick didn't move fast enough for him and Benny mouthed off to Martine. "The talent looks good, but they're not much for direction, are they?"

Martine excused the two of them and steered Benny outside for a chat. Benny was lucky she got to him first. Actors were a touchy bunch, and they all had their own temper triggers. A near universal one was referring to actors as "the talent". Especially to their faces. Benny wouldn't be doing that again. Ever.

The kid came back subdued but not scared off. He gave another set of instructions, much more politely than the last set, and patiently waited for the actors to catch up. During the break when they were rearranging themselves once again, he heard Sydney's breath hitch. "Wait a minute, everyone. Can you give me and Sydney a minute?"

Layla wasn't impressed at the delay, but the rest of them flocked to the craft services area. "Save Sydney some cake!" he yelled after them. Chris waited until Nick acknowledged him before he turned his full attention onto his mistress.

"What's up, Sydney?" he asked her quietly. It wasn't an accusation. He needed this to go better than it was going, but she'd distanced herself from him for some reason. She hadn't held back all day, and the fact she was starting to now was worrisome. He hadn't even done anything wrong this time. When Nick and Sean introduced themselves, he'd peeked through the window and rescued her from her star-struck state as soon as he could. This wasn't star-struck. This was different.

"Nothing, I'm fine," was her immediate response.

"Do you want to try that again?"

"No."

She was a little better now that they were mostly alone.

"Sydney, what's wrong?"

"You're looking at me funny," she told him.

"No, I'm not." He was looking at her, but there was absolutely nothing funny about it. "You're awfully tense," he continued.

"I'm doing the best I can," she whispered. "I'm out of my element, and I can't find my footing. You, I could handle. And I was the boss so you couldn't say anything, anyway. Nick Thurston and Sean Glenn I would have eventually gotten over. But this is…" She waved her hand. "I thought it would just be Benny, and that was bad enough. But there's that other guy, and so many pictures. I feel like I'm some kind of freak."

"You don't look like some kind of freak. You look…" Edible was how he wanted to end that sentence. If it were just the two of them, he might have risked it, but he couldn't chance it with everyone on the set. Sure, the terms of service agreement meant she couldn't come on to him, but the document was meant to be reciprocal. They'd agreed to set it aside, but here was not the place. Chris wished for the umpteenth time that day that he'd met Sydney anywhere else—anywhere he got to be himself. Not at an industry event. Maybe at his sister's birthday party, where he was just a guy who happened to be famous, not someplace where he had to be a celebrity. "You look like gods should be worshiping you."

She smiled, and her shoulders came down a fraction of an inch. "Thanks. Now can you make everyone quit staring at me?"

"They like you. A lot of times guests on set make things awkward. You're polite, and they appreciate it." They did. Sydney was the cute kind of star-struck. It was better than the I'm-an-actor-too-can-you-introduce-me-to-your-agent kind. In the two seasons they'd been filming, they'd also had the creepy kind of star-struck where the actors would be followed around the set and the stalker ignored all concept of personal space and privacy. That kind was the worst.

"They don't all like me," she corrected.

"Who doesn't?"

"Layla."

"Layla is a little temperamental, but she's a professional. Did she say something?"

"I've got twenty bucks that says the toga idea was hers."

Nasty Sydney was new. She was also right. "She comes off a little cool but…"

"Don't try to blow smoke up my ass. Layla's a stone-cold bitch. Hence the toga."

He couldn't argue that assessment, especially if Sydney had actually met her before today. She was right—Layla was a piece of work. The two of them had shown great chemistry at their joint audition, but right after the contracts had been signed, the actress' personality had taken a hundred-and-eighty degree turn into darkness. Nobody on set liked her because although she was always professional, she still managed to be a bigger pain in the ass than the rest of the cast combined. The dislike was mutual; Layla was never invited to non-production events since nobody wanted her around. The cast and crew suffered through her presence only because there was nothing they could do but bribe the writers to kill off her character, and with her fan base that was never going to happen.

That also explained Layla's unexpected generous wardrobe offer. It had been a setup, one obviously designed to upset Sydney. He didn't know the mechanics of the insult, but it had worked. Sydney was definitely upset. He couldn't do anything about it now, but fortunately he had the rest of the season to make her pay, and Nick would be more than willing to help him.

Over her shoulder, Chris saw Nick herding the actors back toward the set. "We'll keep her away from you.

Aside from Layla, is there anything I can do for you?"

"Thanks. I think I'm okay now. All I needed was a minute to find my balance. Just don't disappear on me again, okay?"

"Okay. Are you hungry? We have cake," he said, raising his voice. "Or at least we did. Did you vultures leave our guest of honor any?"

"It was a battle, but I saved her a corner piece. Extra icing," Nick assured him as they resumed their places.

"Do you want me to get it for you?"

Her smile was back when she replied, "You want to let me eat cake? Wouldn't it be more appropriate for you to peel me a grape?"

Chris had no comeback to that. How could he defend himself against Marie Antoinette and Cleopatra in one shot when he'd given her the perfect setup?

"Now," she continued, tapping her foot in exaggerated impatience.

Chris heard something crash behind him. He turned to see that Sean had missed his seat at the banquet table and was laughing his ass off on the floor. Two of the goddesses were a different shade of red as they tried to fight back laughter until they lost it; Layla wore her usual frown. Chris was happy to see his best friend wasn't laughing at him. Poor Nick was as stunned as he was at the quip. Even Martine on the sidelines was in stitches.

Then he clued into Benny's shouts in the background. "Hold it! Hold it!" the photographer shouted as he recorded the scene for posterity.

Chris let the photographer have his fun for a few more shots before he bowed at Sydney. "As my mistress wishes." He took the long route to the table. The one that passed by Robert Clancy.

As he'd hoped, the producer snagged him. "That was

nice work, Chris."

"Thanks."

"Walk me to my car. I'd like to talk to you about something," the man said.

Chris waved at Nick. He pointed at Clancy, then at Sydney, who was attempting to help Sean to his feet. Nick frowned and pointed to his watch. Chris flashed him both hands—ten minutes. Nick frowned again and nodded.

Chris jumped a couple of steps to catch up with the producer. Karma was about to pay off.

Chapter 14

Sydney's stomach rumbled. It had been a long time since her cranberry scone and the piece of cake at her grandmother's hadn't been more than a couple bites. Martine and Nick had dragged her over to a table in the corner stacked with Olympus swag: signed photos, memorabilia, and a couple copies of the show's first season on DVD. Sydney beamed at the PR woman. "This is so great. Thank you!" There was enough stuff for a couple of prize baskets for the benefit this afternoon; it could sell thousands of dollars' worth of extra tickets.

"Chris said it was for a charity? Can you tell me a bit about it?" Martine prompted. She had her phone in her hand with a recording app visible on the screen. Sydney recognized a sound bite opportunity when she saw one. She waited for Martine to give her a go-ahead nod, and she began.

"Curse the Darkness is a charity that helps burn victims get reconstructive surgery. Our biggest annual fundraising events are happening today. This afternoon we are wrapping up our volleyball tournament at Manhattan Beach starting at three o'clock. People and companies have been sponsoring the teams for the last six weeks. We are having the championship match and a silent auction, which is now going to have an awesome Olympus prize. Then tonight is Curse the Darkness' gala, with more raffles, and another Olympus prize, then a bachelor and bachelorette auction." That sounded pretty professional. It was a good thing she and Ashleigh and the rest of the crew had polished and practiced a publicity blurb before the sake the night before. At best they'd hoped they might be able to get some radio play on a small station. "Is this going up on your website?" Sydney asked hopefully.

"Yes. We'll pop it up on our social media sites too. It's short and sweet."

"That would be amazing. Thank you."

Martine leaned in. "Thank you. I hadn't considered tying this into a charity event. You letting us ride your coattails makes us look good."

Sydney's stomach rumbled again, this time loud enough to draw attention.

"Wasn't Chris bringing you some cake?"

"I thought so." He'd vanished on her. Again. At least this time she knew why. He'd touched her back, and he knew which charity she was promoting today. Add in with her panic attack at the thought of wearing a toga, and he had a clear picture. Chris wasn't stupid. She could come up with a dozen reasons why a drop-dead gorgeous movie star wouldn't want to be seen anywhere near her. It hurt, but she wasn't surprised.

Sydney shook it off. It wasn't her fault he was an ass and was proving it to the world. "Would it be okay if I had a piece? It's been a long time since I've eaten and will be even longer until supper." The snack table—craft services table, he'd called it—was loaded with sandwiches and cans of soda.

"Absolutely."

It was tricky to eat and still be able to answer questions from Martine and Nick. Martine's were professional. Nick wanted the dirt on what she'd made Chris do as her slave. Sydney dished a little but held back any mention of the melon incident. Chris may not worry about karma, but she did. She did go into excruciating detail about Chris almost landing on his ass to get away from the pooper scooper. Sydney didn't even mind Benny popping in and out of view as her hands flew to illustrate the story.

She was actually having a good chat with them when her watch beeped. She checked it, and then double-checked the time on her phone. It was five minutes to two. Already. "Thank you so much for everything. The baskets are incredibly generous. I can't believe it's time to go. Do you have a place I can get changed?"

"Can't you stay?" Martine gave a half-hearted attempt to wheedle some more shots, but with her knowledge of Sydney's plans and the fact the show was now involved in the fundraiser, she didn't push it.

Neither mentioned the obvious fact the sweepstakes prize was AWOL and had been for some time. Sydney swung between disappointed and devastated. Setting aside the flirting altogether, which she was loathe to do, she'd believed Chris would have at least made an effort to keep up his side of their bargain. Still, his friends were honoring their parts, and she had things to do.

Nick walked her to the limo to get her bag. "So Layla and I will be coming to the beach with you and Chris, if that's all right."

"It's great. But I think it might be just the three of us. Chris vanished about twenty minutes ago. Can you call him?" Sydney asked.

She could have sworn a frown flickered across Nick's face, but he agreed and was dialing when she ducked into the empty trailer he delivered her to. Sydney slipped the dress onto the hanger and into the garment bag she'd folded into her duffel. The sandals came off, as did the fancy slip and bra underneath. She fought and fumbled with the racer-back sports support until everything was where it should be in the reinforced bra. Damn, the things were effective, but women had to be half-octopus to get them on. Sydney rarely wore them;

the shoulder straps aggravated her skin, but on the beach it would beat the alternative. The Veggie Delights were a wonderfully vicious duo made up of the previous night's other sake victims. She and Ashleigh had played them twice before, and they'd each won once. She'd need every advantage she could get, starting with her outfit. The board shorts and fitted T-shirt finished her conversion into a beach bum. Sydney washed most of the makeup off and pulled her hair back into the Pebbles Flintstone ponytail she'd started the morning with.

When she stepped out of the trailer, Nick was coming out of his own next door. He'd changed into beach clothes as well. "That was fast," he said.

"Did you find Chris?"

"Um…"

That would be a "no". She'd say this for him—he deserved the role. She'd been completely taken in by Chris' acting skills. He was very good at his job.

It was tempting to call Ashleigh up and start badmouthing him to everyone in earshot, but he had gotten her a couple prize packs and some publicity for her events today. For a couple hours of her day, Sydney was willing to call it a fair trade.

Nick hesitated at the door to the limo. "Let's give him a couple more minutes."

"No. He knows—um, knew—I have to leave now. We need to get rolling." She'd given him enough.

Nick nodded reluctantly. He jogged over to the soundstage and spoke to somebody hidden behind the door. Benny darted right through the open vehicle door and sat close to the driver's window. Layla Andrews appeared dressed to kill. She looked good, but Sydney allowed herself a smile at the thought of those shoes being destroyed once they hit rough pavement and then sand. Layla was halfway to the limo when Nick finally emerged with Sean Glenn in tow.

"I'm sorry. We can't find Chris," Nick informed her.

"I'm not surprised," both she and Layla replied in unison. Even worse, they said it for the same reason, and Layla, damn her, seemed to know it.

The redhead threw himself against the back bench. "There'll be chicks at this thing, right?"

"Chicks in bikinis," she promised, then laughed when he relaxed into the seat. None of the chicks she knew would be in bikinis, but it was volleyball on a beach in California. At least one woman had to be wearing one, despite the February weather.

She excused herself and started a flurry of texts to Ashleigh, discussing the raffle baskets, Chris' abscondment, and how to spread the word that Ares, Hera, and Eros would be around for photos and autographs—at least for a few minutes—when they arrived. Sydney's head popped up at one of her friend's suggestions.

"I know you all don't intend to hang out long, and I appreciate you coming at all. But if you did want to watch the game, my friend can arrange some seating with our guests of honor. There's a private section on the sidelines where some of our charity recipients will be sitting," she offered.

"No, thank you. I'll show up and do my part, but I'm not comfortable being around sick people," Layla said.

"Of course. Your comfort at an event for burn victims is my primary concern." She should have simply refused Layla's offer to attend in the first place. Sydney's VIPs would never pass Hollywood's entrance requirements, even after surgery. Sydney knew their self-consciousness could be fought but never completely conquered. They didn't need someone like Layla reminding them of it and making them feel bad about themselves.

"I'll watch," Sean said. "My cousin plays on the national circuit."

"Cool. We aren't that good, but it will be a fun game."

Nick shrugged. "I'm waiting to hear back on plans, but I'll hang around until I do." He frowned, and Sydney saw the wheels turning. "We should have grabbed Russ. And some guys from security."

Neither she nor Ashleigh had considered that. Why would they? It wasn't a problem for them. Her face must have said as much because he waved her off. "Never mind," he continued, "I'll call him now."

"Where is Chris anyway? You didn't scare him off somehow, did you?" Layla asked.

"Maybe it was the thought of spending time with you." Dear God, that made it past her internal Mute button. Sydney bit her tongue, returned to her phone, and ignored the silence in the car.

Unfortunately, Layla was right. She had run Chris off. She'd seen him with his dates on various media outlets. She was never going to be movie star material, and she was okay with that. It was one thing for Chris to be photographed with someone like her for a contest or charity event. It was another for him to be seen out with her voluntarily. Gods like him and mere mortals like her were a bad idea.

The fantastic Mr. Banks started making a series of turns and slowed to a stop at the curb of Ocean Drive. Sydney sent a final "we're here" text and slipped the phone into her bag.

"Can you give security some time to catch up?" Nick

asked.

"Of course."

It didn't take that long. Apparently, the limo had caught the tail end of a traffic accident tie up. The chase car hadn't had any problems getting to the beach in record time. A burly arm knocked on the limousine window almost immediately.

Nick smiled. "That's Russ. We're good to go."

Sydney grabbed the closest basket of goodies and tucked them into the crook of one arm. She was reaching for the second one when Sean grabbed it. "I've got this one."

"Thanks. Are you ready for this?" she asked them all.

She was blinded with bleached teeth smiles and nearly drowned in the exuded feel-good vibes. It was one man short of perfect.

Chapter 15

The set visit had gone phenomenally well. Aside from Sydney being overwhelmed by the photographers, the only other hiccup had been when Martine warned him off about being too handsy with Sydney outside his trailer. He suspected she was concerned about him violating the terms of service and the lawsuits that could follow, but he and Sydney had already covered that ground.

Chris was trying not to smile too hard. He didn't want to put out the wrong vibe. Or seem too eager, although it was too late for that one. He was walking Robert Clancy to his car because the man who had his finger in four of the biggest blockbusters in the last two years wanted to discuss something with him. Karma was so worth it. He promised to help Sydney with her fundraiser, and it was going to reap him the leading man role. All he had to do was take a quick stroll and return with cake to celebrate and say thanks for her help. He might even have a piece. He stuck his hand into his pocket and turned off his phone. He only had a few minutes.

Then he realized that Clancy had spoken. Crap, he couldn't let himself be distracted now. "I'm sorry, what was that?"

"You looked distracted so I asked what was on your mind," Clancy said.

"Sydney's cake," he replied without thinking. "Before I ran into you I promised I'd get her some," he rambled, sure he sounded like an idiot.

The producer laughed. "I was watching you two. You did a great job calming her down during the shoot. It says a lot that you're willing to work on a publicity stunt like this. It was a bold idea that could have gone either way."

A modicum of modesty would be appropriate. "I got lucky with Sydney."

"I heard there was a mix-up when you first arrived. She wasn't expecting you?" Clancy asked.

Chris had no idea how the man got that information, but it offered him a wedge. "She wasn't, but she was a little star-struck. All she needed was a little guidance." He was going to hell for that. Him guide her? Sydney had run him ragged from the minute she'd opened the door the second time. The producer smiled at his proclamation of leadership. "I knew the opportunity the sweepstakes could have for the show. Even though Sydney was a little unhelpful earlier on, I knew I'd be able to compensate for her." He couldn't stop his mouth from spewing the derogatory remarks. "Of course, when I found out she was volunteering at a charity event it was a no-brainer to get involved, although I must admit that Martine should get a lot of the credit for getting it set up so quickly at the last minute." And the rest should go to Nick because God knew Chris sure as hell didn't do the work.

"How is Sydney to work with?"

His ego overrode his brain. "She's, well, sweet. She's no actress, but I'm doing my best. To tell you the truth, I volunteered for this to use it to get High Note's attention. I probably could have done better with someone more…Hollywood, but I think I'm doing pretty well with what I have to work with. This contest is going to bump the show to the next level when it comes to social media," he bragged. "But I'll be glad when it's done and I'm back to working with professionals." Chris shut down the part of his brain that was screaming his commentary was a bad idea. As long as the producer was smiling, he wasn't going to stop.

Clancy nodded. "Your winner looks like she can be challenging, but what I've seen so far today has impressed me. We need a lead that can generate that kind of chemistry in a short time for our new project."

"I've heard that you've already started to cast."

It was a dance. Who'd heard what, who needed what, who offered what. Chris walked Clancy to his car, where they chatted about the project in general. Then he got into the passenger seat to continue their conversation. Clancy fired up the climate control and left the luxury sedan in park, and they took a few minutes to get into specifics. Really good specifics. They called Chris' agent and got the ball rolling. It was not at all the way the business usually went, but Chris sure as hell wasn't going to argue. Karma was finally on his side, and he wasn't going to rock the boat.

Robert Clancy was actually a pretty nice guy. It was above and beyond for him to do this deal in person on a Saturday when he was supposed to be off work. "It would be premature to go out and celebrate, but you might want to start planning something for after you're through with Sydney," the producer said with a grin.

"I'm working on something already as a matter of fact."

"Good luck with that. But I should let you go. I didn't mean to keep you as long as I did, and it's never right to keep a pretty lady waiting."

Chris shook his head. "Sydney's really good about stuff like this."

He shook the producer's hand and climbed out, waving goodbye as the producer pulled out of the lot. Then he took the direct route back to the soundstage but didn't put on any speed. Martine was going to need a few minutes to show Sydney the charity stuff she'd arranged. The studio had gotten lucky with that one. The sweepstakes winner was getting all kinds of crap anyway. Throwing in some extra stuff for the sweepstakes winner's charity was sweet PR icing on both Martine's and Sydney's cakes that nobody was going to argue about.

It was an easy walk back to the soundstage. He didn't think anything of the empty street until he walked onto the set and all he found were a couple PAs clearing off the remaining food in the craft services area. The rest of the cast was long gone. He swept the area and found Martine sitting in a chair, shoes off, massaging her instep.

"Did you move the shoot?" he asked.

"What shoot?"

"Sydney's shoot. The sweepstakes shoot. The one you didn't warn me about but I got us here for anyway," Chris elaborated. Now he was starting to feel bad. Sydney was uncomfortable enough on set. If she got dragged to somewhere else on the lot, he was not going to be happy. Sure, Nick would watch out for her; the guy felt guilty when he realized his surprise had almost screwed Syd over. But it was Chris' job to keep an eye on her, and he didn't want someone else stepping in, even for a few minutes.

"Oh, you mean the shoot that ended an hour ago," Martine sniped. She slipped her stilettos back on and stood in his personal space. "The one you disappeared from without warning? The 'slave for a day' one we finished without the slave? It went pretty well, no thanks to you."

The blonde was crazy. "An hour ago? I've been gone for fifteen minutes."

She swept her arm around the building. "Get a clue,

Chris. We're ready to lock up and turn out the lights. The show's over. I can't believe you blew that poor girl off like that. Dick move. She was such a sweetie too. You can't imagine how big you owe Nicky for stepping in."

The place was deserted, but there was no way he was gone for an hour. Chris pulled out his phone and turned it on. The speaker erupted in a never-ending barrage of voicemail and text message notifications. The clock at the bottom of the screen showed a shocking "2:24 p.m.". Chris snapped his arm out and pushed back the cuff. His watch confirmed it.

God damn it to hell. He couldn't have taken that long with Robert Clancy. Five minutes to walk there, five minutes back, they talked for a bit, then the call with his agent, which ran for ten, maybe fifteen…Oh, crap. "When did she leave?"

"Half an hour ago-ish. She's long gone. I doubt anyone can get that woman off-schedule. Did you know she organized the whole fundraiser for her Change the Darkness day?"

"Curse the Darkness," Chris corrected. He could get Sydney off-schedule. All he'd have to do was lie to her again. Not much, just enough to mess up a day she'd been planning for months. "Please tell me she at least got the gifts we promised. And that Nick went with her."

"Nicky went with her. So did Layla, Benny, and Sean. They took two gift baskets. We closed the sweepstakes site when she left. It was supposed to stay open until sunset, per the advertising, but with you gone we didn't have an option," Martine told him. She tucked a lock of her blonde hair behind her ear. "So you're sprung for the day."

"I don't want to be sprung!" He wanted to push the clock back half an hour. Shit. He should have told

Sydney where he was going. Or asked Clancy if they could meet the next day because he had to honor the sweepstakes contract. Hell, Clancy could have worked the whole deal through Chris' agent.

Chris would have preferred he had. That impulsiveness his agent hated so much had reared its ugly head again. It was entirely possible Chris had weakened his position after his unguarded conversation with Clancy. A few thoughtless comments he'd made about his experiences today echoed in his head now. He wished them back now because if they ever made their way back to Sydney he wasn't sure he'd be able to look her in the eyes again.

The irony was, because of the time he'd spent making them, he might not get the chance to anyway.

Martine dismissed his claim with a wave. "At least you know we'll never ask you to do it again. You looked pretty enough in the pictures, but I thought you'd show a little more class than you did. Hell, you volunteered for it. We'll know better next time."

"If you shut down the sweepstakes page, why'd you send Benny?"

"Studio site. Charity function. We're lucky she still let us tag along after we announced you were going to be there."

"Look," he pleaded. "I'll get myself down there. I'll finish being the contest prize. Keep the sweepstakes site running."

Martine stared him down. "Why? Do you have any idea how pissed your girl was? She only did the shoot on the condition you'd help her out, and then you disappeared. If your castmates hadn't covered your ass, the show would be screwed. She's not going to give you another chance to give yourself good press. I don't blame her."

"She could. She will. I can convince her." He had to or he could lose everything. The image in his head of a marquee sign with his name in lights faded into a picture of him escorting Sydney into her gala that evening. He'd be back in his tuxedo. She'd be wearing an evening gown that revealed only enough to get his imagination revving. He tried to hold on to that image, but it faded into Sydney giving him the look she'd given him at the Dobsons', the one where she was sure he was going to disappoint her.

He hadn't then. He'd saved it until it really counted.

Chris had no idea karma worked so damn fast.

Chapter 16

All a girl needed was a BFF she could count on. Ashleigh was hers. The event was in full swing when she arrived a little after half past two. Sydney spotted the usual suspects around the volleyball court, shilling raffle tickets to an enormous crowd. The prize bundles were lined up on a table with three charity staffers making sure the draws were set to go smoothly before the game. She set her Olympus basket in the prominent spot they'd left open for her and was nearly trampled by ticket holders. Sydney handed the spare off to a traitorous volunteer wearing a Team Veggie Delight shirt, who took off to lock it in his car until the silent auction that evening.

Ashleigh pulled her out of the way. "My girl parties with the gods," her friend whispered as she stared at the trio of actors and the studio security who'd met them there. Nick Thurston and Sean Glenn glad-handed the crowd and posed with the ladies. Layla Andrews was content to be photographed alone and condescended to be in a few shots with a couple of good-looking men she pulled from the crowd.

"I don't party with them. The show made them come."

"Uh-huh. Smile!" Ashleigh wrapped her arm around Sydney's waist and beamed at Benny, who appeared in front of them, camera up.

Sydney froze. "Wait, try again!" she said to Benny's disappointed face when he looked at the camera's display screen.

This time they were both ready. Benny took the shot and promised them copies. By the time he was back to taking pictures of the crowd, Ashleigh had tugged Sydney over to the sideline. "I have a surprise for you."

"I've had enough surprises today, thanks."

"You'll open it, and you'll like it," Ashleigh ordered.

"Fine." Sydney opened the bag and pulled out a racer-back tank top with "Team Scar" screen-printed on the front. There was no chance in hell. "I can't wear that."

"You can, and you will. For pictures at least," Ashleigh insisted.

"I really can't."

Ashleigh grabbed her shoulders and twisted until Sydney faced the temporary bleachers cordoned off on the other side of the court. The first two rows consisted of men in military haircuts all sporting tank tops with identical logos. Half of them were obviously wounded warriors, bandages and scars on display and visible under the shirts. Ashleigh lifted the shirt in her hand over her head and shook it in the air. The crowd went nuts, shouting words of encouragement to the pair that made up Team Scar.

"That's low, Ash."

"I know. It's also necessary. It's time, Sydney."

"Easy for you to say."

"No. It's not."

It probably wasn't. Ashleigh had been there for her through every minute of her stay in the burn ward, through all her rehab, and there for her again through the surgeries and rehab after that. She knew Sydney's state of mind about the scars on her back and shoulder. The doctors and Sydney's family had promised that the scarring was much better than it had been, but whenever she looked in the mirror it was like the first time she'd seen herself after the accident. It was Ashleigh who made her believe the truth.

Sydney blushed hard. "I haven't told you why Chris

didn't show up."

"He's a movie star. I figured he flaked. Enough said. At least his buddies showed up."

"He didn't flake. He found out about my burns and disappeared."

The temperature around them dropped ten degrees. "Excuse me?" Ashleigh demanded.

She'd been wrong. This was what BFFs were for. Sydney recounted every word of the toga fiasco, every touch Chris had given her until his hand hit the scars under the material of her dress, and his subsequent, immediate disappearance.

Ashleigh turned and stared daggers at Layla until Sydney spun her back around. "Fuck Chris. Fuck that bitch. You are so much more than both of them. Show them both they can go to hell."

"People will stare," Sydney whispered.

"People are looking at the guys," Ashleigh replied quietly.

That was different. Who would insult a war hero?

Ashleigh raised the tank and shook it again. Another roar of approval crashed over Sydney.

"You're beautiful, and fuck anybody who says otherwise. You can do this, Syd."

Each breath took a lifetime as Sydney grabbed the hem of her T-shirt and lifted it past her belly and then her shoulders. She tugged the collar over her head and stood frozen in her sports bra, right on the beach where everyone could see her. Ashleigh had to pry her shirt out of her grip.

Sydney dropped the tank once as she tried to put it on. Ashleigh left the T-shirt on the ground and grabbed both of Sydney's hands. "Breathe. You're doing great." She lifted Sydney's hand and inhaled with an exaggerated breath, then exhaled the same way. Sydney mimicked her until she remembered how to do it on her own.

It took two tries to get her head and arms through the right holes, but she did get the tank top on. Only as she straightened the seams running down the sides did she realize how quiet everyone had become. When she turned to face the bleachers, everyone she knew in the crowd erupted in applause.

"You are amazing," Ashleigh whispered in her ear as she crushed her in a hug.

"You, too." It was a good thing Ashleigh was holding her up because she wouldn't have managed on her own. She finally let her friend go and waved to her fans, pointing proudly at the logo on her chest.

The referee approached them from across the sand. "Ladies, we're going to get started in about ten minutes. I know you wanted to have a word first."

This was Sydney's department. It was another pre-sake speech her crew had helped her prepare. This one was so important they'd even written it down. She'd have to amend it to say thanks to the actress and actors who'd come along and who were, by the looks of it, raking it in hand over fist as they sold tickets in front of the prize table. Well, the guys were selling tickets. Layla stood by the baskets like a statue.

Sydney jogged over to them, wishing she'd worn her ponytail lower so she could pull it over her shoulder. "Sorry, everyone, I need to steal the Greeks for a moment." For the most part the crowd let them go with some half-hearted groans. A few pushy Olympus fans had to be held back as Sydney drew them away and explained she was going to mention them in the game's opening remarks. The guys were cool with it. She wasn't surprised when Layla kicked up a fuss.

"I'll stand up there with you, but could you at least put your shirt back on?"

Sydney flinched. Even Sean's jaw dropped at the blatant insult, and he'd been spotlighted in the press for his inappropriate remarks in the past. Nick opened his mouth to defend her, but someone beat him to it.

"What did you say?" Chris asked from behind her.

This was all Sydney needed. Her day hadn't been complete until the guy who dropped her for her scars came to her rescue for being damaged. She'd been a good person for most of her life. She'd definitely treated Chris better than he deserved. How had she managed to piss karma off so badly? She should have told the whole world about the melons if this was how her life was going to play out. "What are you doing here?" Sydney asked.

"One second, Syd. Layla, what did you just say?" Chris repeated.

"Looking at her back makes me uncomfortable," the actress said.

"Guilt does that," Ashleigh snapped.

"Jesus, Layla—" Chris began.

"Oh, please, like you didn't disappear the second you felt the scars under my dress," Sydney spat in his face.

"What?"

"You heard me. You were all huggy and arms around me for the pictures until you touched my back. You couldn't get far enough away after that. Then you vanished altogether."

"Not true."

"I was there," she argued.

"I'm trying to help you here."

"Shut up, Chris!" the women shouted in stereo.

Sydney turned on Layla. "You didn't need me to take off my shirt to know exactly how my back looks. It's funny how you can't deal with it here but were willing to have me show it off in front of all your coworkers. Did you plan to insult me there, too, or drown me in sympathy until I died of embarrassment?"

"I'd deny that the toga was my idea, but you'd never believe me," Layla said.

"Damn straight! Your word is as good as his," Sydney shot back, pointing at Chris even as she pulled away from him. She didn't need defending, and she definitely didn't need it from him. There was no way she was going to cower in front of that poisonous bitch.

"You can't say that!" Layla dug in her purse, and Sydney knew she was going for a phone.

"I didn't say anything. And I've got witnesses. What are you going to tell them? Besides, you started it!" It was a juvenile comeback but utterly appropriate. The list of things the two of them weren't allowed to say about the accident per the lawyers and the judge was lengthy. They probably shouldn't be talking at all. Right now she didn't care. In fact, she turned her back to Layla. "Take a good look. This is my burn scar. It hurt like hell. And it is why we're here. You agreed to be here, and you knew damned well what to expect before you showed up. If you don't want to hang around after, we'll do your part and you can leave. But I'm—we're—not going to hide to protect your delicate sensibilities. Conversation over."

Nick and Sean smiled broadly for Benny as she posed with the Olympus crew for some group shots before the game. Sydney's grin was full of bravado. She didn't look at Chris or Layla. They could be as uncomfortable as they wanted while they stood beside her exposed shoulder.

As soon as Benny was done, Ashleigh tossed her shirt at her.

"Syd, you don't need to cover up because of what Layla said. And you definitely don't have to for me," Chris said.

"Not everything is about you, Chris," she retorted as she pulled the tee over her head. His arrogance knew no bounds. The shirt wasn't to protect her from the looks she was getting; it was to protect her tender skin from the sun and the sand.

Sydney left Chris arguing with his castmate as she stomped through the sand to the boxes piled at the sideline. She accepted the referee's hand up and called for attention. "Thanks, everyone, for coming to the final death match of the Curse the Darkness Beach Volleyball Tournament where the most awesome and amazing Team Scar, consisting of me, Sydney Richardson, and Ashleigh Jessup, is going to pound the totally-unworthy-despite-being-tied-with-us-for-points Team Veggie Delight into the sand. Veggies, do you want to wave?" Sydney pointed across the court. "That's Caitlin Kelly and Vanessa Vaughn, the official opposition." Both teams were cheered on by the onlookers.

"And we have two sets of special guests. In the bleachers, from the best care center in Los Angeles with the best-looking patients as well as some friends in uniform, is Curse the Darkness' tremendous cheering section and reason we're here. Can we please show these incredible people our support?"

When the guys looked annoyed at the attention, Sydney laughed at them. "Payback, it's a...five letter word that rhymes with bitch." The crowd roared again. Then she swept her arm to the other side of the court. "We are also very lucky to have some of the stars of Olympus here to lend their support. And they brought a gift basket so buy tickets! I'd like to introduce the most generous Nick 'Ares' Thurston and Sean 'Eros' Glenn. Beside them is Layla 'Hera' Andrews. Oh, and Chris 'Zeus' Peck is back there too. Thank you guys so much for coming out and helping to raise funds for a really great cause." Her thanks was begrudged but genuine. The crowd was small but still tons larger than it would have been if the show hadn't gotten the foundation's name out there. If every person bought five dollars' worth of tickets, it would be a couple extra thousand dollars raised. Despite the fact two of the four stars attending were assholes, it was still good they came.

"The prize table is going to draw tickets and post the winning numbers in a few minutes, so please go and see if you've won a prize from any of our fantastic sponsors, whose logos are liberally sprinkled around the area. They are great people. Go spend your money in their stores and restaurants! And in the meantime, it's time to get down to business. Ladies, on the court!"

Sydney joined Ashleigh on the court. They approached the net and ducked under it to speak to the opposition without being heard.

"How are you feeling?" Vanessa asked her like she hadn't been sitting across the table from her the night before.

"Sake is evil," Sydney replied with a smirk. Vanessa had to be hurting more than she was.

"Sing it, sister," Vanessa's black-haired partner Caitlin agreed.

"And it's the two all-girl teams in the final. I told you so," Ashleigh threw out.

"Yeah, you called it," Vanessa said. "Now stop yapping and let's get this show on the road."

The women high-fived each other and took their places. Sydney specifically didn't look to the bleachers where Chris, Nick, Sean, and Benny were now sitting among the guys from the VA. Russ had put Layla into a car after her speech. Nobody missed her. But now Sydney had bigger fish to fry. It was game time.

Chapter 17

Benny was wrong when he said Sydney had shut Chris down quickly on her front step that morning. This was shutting him down fast. Fast and hard and permanent. Chris' mother was a school teacher, and even after twenty-some years of hearing the same advice, he was still learning to not enter a conversation halfway through. This time he really wished he'd paid attention because a four-foot-eleven Filipino actress and a five-foot-five SoCal call center employee could verbally body-slam even the king of the gods.

What he needed was a few minutes of quiet to come up with a game plan to apologize to Sydney. The sweepstakes promo was over in a couple of hours, but he didn't want it to end with her thinking he was an asshole who'd left her in the lurch when he found out her back was scarred. It didn't sound any better to say he left her for totally different, selfish reasons, but her thinking he found her physically repulsive tore at him. It was so far from the truth. He couldn't imagine doing something like that to her. Evidently though, she could. Yeah, he was never going to see her again, but he didn't want his last memory of Sydney to be of her hating him.

The problem was he wasn't going to get a few quiet minutes on the bleachers. Nick was talking to the vets in the front row about Sydney winning the contest. She had more fans than the show did in this crowd. From what he overheard, she knew most of them from the burn ward when she was a patient. His stomach dropped even further. He'd screwed over a charity worker and a burn victim. There was no coming back from karma that bad. His sole saving grace was that although everyone had seen the argument, nobody seemed to have heard what it was about.

Hell, he barely knew what it was about. He got his part. It was bullshit, but he understood how it looked to everyone else. He had no idea how Layla came into it. She obviously knew Sydney was burned long before the sweepstakes ever came into play. And evidently there were lawyers on speed dial, likely involving a gag order because as much as Sydney and Layla had said, there had been a tremendous lack of detail.

That was for later. Figuring out how to get Sydney to listen to him for thirty seconds again was his primary concern. Chris couldn't even ask his friends for help. First of all, he'd already used up all his favors with Nick. Secondly, his remaining co-star was otherwise occupied.

Beside him, Sean seemed really into the game. A little too into it for the beefy African-American guy in a sling sitting in the next row. "Dude, you'd better not be drooling over my sister," the guy in the navy cap growled.

"Which one's your sister?" Sean shot back with a grin.

"Vanessa. Team Veggie Delight."

Chris elbowed Sean in the ribs hard enough to leave a dent. If that didn't give the Greek god of love a hint not to hit on the sailor's little sister, Sean deserved to get pummeled.

"She's very pretty, but I'm more interested in her partner. That Kelly girl's got skills."

"Caitlin's practically my sister," the guy added.

"No, real skills," Sean protested. "My cousin is on the pro circuit. She's really good. She could do damage with those spikes."

"Yeah, she's good," the sailor agreed. He offered Sean his hand. "Trent Vaughn."

Sean shook it respectfully and introduced himself, and then pointed out and named the others from the show. It went fine until Russ spoke up. "Sean, I don't know if you want to sit by a guy who was too dumb to duck."

"Fuck you, asshole," Trent shot back to Russ.

Oh hell no! His bodyguard was not going to ruin the goodwill the show was generating with the foundation by insulting the wounded men and women who were Sydney's friends and supporters. He had enough problems today. "Mr. Vaughn, Trent, my friend Russ didn't mean to suggest…"

Trent waved him off with a laugh. "Relax. I served with this bozo from back in the day. He wasn't any more PC back then."

Okay, good to know. None of the other veterans seemed offended either. It must be one of those navy things. Sometimes he forgot Russ had a career before the show. They always called him a drill sergeant and referred to him as ex-navy, but that was just a line on his resume to Chris. Now he realized his fight trainer was sitting among his brothers in arms. It hit him that Sydney's charity was more than convenient for the show; it mattered to people he knew, people he was friends with. He was glad he got a chance to participate in this. Sydney had given him more than she'd ever know.

Chris took a few deep breaths to get his blood pressure below aneurysm level after Russ' comment and tried to regain his train of thought on the "apologize to Sydney" plan-making front. He didn't get far.

"Damn! Great block!" Sean yelled at the court.

Sean must have been impressed. He was notorious as a horn-dog, both as himself and as the character he played. Chris couldn't remember the last time Sean had looked at a female without the next words out of his mouth being some kind of innuendo or invitation. Except when he'd met Sydney. Probably because Sean knew that Martine would go up one side of him and down the other, and that Chris would stomp on whatever was left.

"Caitlin's an actress, you know," Trent said to Russ. The man spoke low. If conversation in the stands hadn't died off for that split second, Chris never would have heard the comment. It didn't sound like a hint for a job offer to his friend, more like a big brother's brag.

Maybe he could talk to someone at the show and use this as an olive branch...

Use this. Use Sydney's friend. No wonder karma kept kicking him in the balls. "I'm an asshole," Chris muttered as he dropped his head into his hands.

"What, buddy?" Nick asked.

"I'm an asshole. Sydney did nothing but help me out today, and I screwed her over."

Nick pulled his attention from his phone, which he dropped back into his pocket. "No, you didn't. You promised to get her here on time and support her fundraising. She's here. You're here. We're here. And we definitely helped them raise some money. You did your share. She can't expect anything more. It's not like you're dating."

Chris said nothing.

Nick leaned closer to his ear. "You didn't do something stupid like ask her out, did you?"

"Not exactly. I flirted though."

"She's a big girl. She had to know it was for show."

"I flirted with intent. After I told her she couldn't flirt with me because of the sweepstakes' rule. Then I hinted I'd take her to her gala tonight."

"And then you vanished on her? You are an

asshole."

"I meant it!"

Nick leaned in. "Tell me you didn't stop flirting when you found out she was a burn victim. Because these guys will rip you to pieces, and you'd have it coming. In case you haven't noticed, they think the sun shines out of her ass."

After spending six great hours with her, Chris wasn't sure it didn't. "Of course not. The flirting was just for fun at first. When I realized it was getting a bit out of control, I backed off." He was such a liar. When it got serious, Sydney hesitated. He'd started hinting for a date.

"So why did you disappear for so long? Clancy?" Nick asked.

Chris nodded. It hadn't been because of a scar, that was for damned sure. He'd disappeared with no explanation to further his career and then got caught up in the details. That didn't sound any better so he held his tongue. At least his friend waited for the lame explanation he had.

Nick had to let him go when they were pulled to their feet. The tournament was over. The women traded hugs as Team Scar was declared victorious. Chris let himself be swept along with the wave that assembled on the court to congratulate the players.

The losing team was excited to meet the stars of Olympus. They were pulled into several shots with their security team standing by. Chris smirked when he saw Sean catch Trent Vaughn's glare, and then move from having an arm wrapped around each woman to standing beside Nick, not touching either of them.

It was different when they posed with Team Scar. Chris hadn't arrived that late, but it was late enough that Sydney would have had a chance to catch her girlfriend up on his behavior. Nick and Sean got all the love from the duo. Benny insisted he stand beside Sydney for pictures "for the sweepstakes page". Chris got as close as he could, but Ashleigh's arm was wrapped around her friend's shoulder tightly with Sydney's arm looped around her waist. It took him a minute to realize that their casual hug actually protected Sydney's back from the photographer even though it was covered. When Benny was done, Chris got two sets of cool but genuine words of thanks, but it was obvious Sydney considered their agreement fulfilled. He'd been dismissed. Screw that.

He cornered her as she finished congratulating the gift basket winners who had waited until after the game to pick up their prizes. The efficiency of her crew impressed him; most signs of their event were already removed. "Can I talk to you for a second?"

"Sure. What can I do for you?" The "now" was silent.

"Can I apologize?"

"Absolutely." Sydney crossed her arms and waited.

Had he really expected this to go easy? "I didn't feel anything under your dress when we were horsing around with Nicky. I had no idea you'd been hurt until I saw you in your tank top here. Whatever else you think of me, I didn't know you had a burn scar, and I don't care. Cover it, don't cover it, do whatever makes you feel comfortable but never think it makes a difference to me. I have fucked things up from the second we met, but none of it had anything to do with how you look."

It was honest. Horribly phrased but all true. Something flickered in Sydney's eyes but vanished before he could identify it.

"Thank you," she said. It was obvious it cost her, but she said it.

"About me disappearing on the set. Robert Clancy wanted to talk to me…"

Sydney cut him off. "Chris, I think I've hit my limit for apologies and explanations. We should quit while things are relatively decent between us."

"I don't want us to quit."

She dropped her head back and stared at the sky, probably either praying for patience or a lightning bolt to strike him down. When she looked at him again, he guessed lightning bolt. "Your producer guy talked to you so I'm assuming you either got the role or know you're in the running. I've more than done my part. What else do you want from me?"

"I want to make it up to you," was what he settled on. He wanted so much more.

"Why?" she exploded. "What did I do to deserve this today? Seriously? Who did I piss off?"

Her outburst caught Ashleigh's attention. Her friend stomped across the court in their direction. He was running out of time.

"Why? I expected today to be an absolute disaster, and then I met you. You're sarcastic and funny and generous and beautiful, and you give me shit when I screw up and, fuck me, but I like it. I like you, Sydney. A lot," Chris said in a rush. "Arguments aside, and we had a lot, this was the best time I've had in ages. Didn't you think so?"

"Of course you had a good time. You got everything you wanted."

"One more chance, Syd. Please. Three will be the charm, I promise."

Ashleigh stepped between them. "You okay, Syd? Is he causing problems?"

"He apologized," Sydney told her.

He refused to flinch under Ashleigh's inspection. So much had been given to him for so long that he'd almost forgotten what it was like to earn something worthwhile. This was worthwhile.

"What are we going to do with his apology?" Ashleigh asked.

"I'm not sure yet."

"Does he want something?"

He could answer that. "I want to make it up to her. Me almost kidnapping her and leaving her at the studio and being late here. All of it."

"And you'd get what out of it?" Ashleigh pressed.

Best friend wrath. Nothing like it. "Nothing. I've taken way too much from Sydney today. All I want is to spend a little time with her on her terms." He'd burned Ashleigh as well when he broke his promise. He'd gotten, well, Sydney had gotten herself to the beach on time, but Chris had promised he'd show up to help fundraise and he hadn't. Money, fame, the power of being the ruler of Olympus—none of it helped him now.

"Well, you can't have her right now," Ashleigh told them. "We need you back on the court, Syd."

The comment shook Sydney out of her funk. "Why? What's wrong?"

A small smile broke through Ashleigh's anger. "His guys"—she nodded at Chris—"challenged our guys to a grudge match."

Chris looked back to the bleachers. Sean had pulled his shirt off and was basking in the glow of fans on the sidelines while he and Nick stretched. The veterans in the bleachers were amped up; trash talk between the actors and the people in the stands floated over to them.

"I don't know if that's a good idea, Ash."

"Too late," Ashleigh chirped. "It's a done deal. Our

VIPs ponied up five hundred dollars for the girls' side. The Olympus guys each pledged to match it."

"Who's playing?" Chris asked.

"Sydney and Caitlin."

"They volunteered me?" Sydney squeaked.

"And Caitlin. Well, Trent volunteered Caitlin because apparently Sean Glenn was talking about her and she picked you as her partner."

"Do people not realize that I'm busy today?" Sydney asked the universe.

Chris understood her point. It made him feel worse. He wasn't the only one who'd taken advantage of her. The hits kept coming, and Sydney stayed standing. She impressed the hell out of him. He'd been lucky he got to her first. But maybe he could help her now, if only a little bit. "I'll put five hundred on you and Caitlin."

"In exchange for what?"

That burned. "As a thank you for hearing me out. Nothing more. What do you say, Syd?"

The redhead in front of him pulled out her ponytail, re-gathered her hair, and tied it back again. Then she shrugged. "I don't know, Chris." Sydney started to lope across the sand.

It wasn't a no. He'd take it.

Chapter 18

Sydney wasn't much for swearing, but an Internet acronym crossed her mind that was perfect for this situation: FML. Fuck my life. An apologetic Greek god on one side, wounded warriors screaming for victory on the other, exposing her scars to the world behind her, and a vital gala she had to get ready for looming this evening. FML fit her perfectly.

Suck it up, buttercup. This would all be over by dawn, and she wouldn't have to worry about fundraising for another nine months. Today was important; she knew firsthand how worthwhile it was. This challenge match was one more thing on her never-ending list, but it was doable. Volleyball first, then gala. She'd decide about Chris when and if she wanted to.

She was halfway across the court when she stopped dead. Then she ran back to Chris, who was making his way around the court to the bleachers. "Did you get it?"

"Get what?"

"The part. From that Clancy guy."

"Unofficially, yes."

She didn't know what to do with that answer now that she had it so she left him on the sidelines and raced over to Caitlin, Nick, and Sean.

Her fellow sake victim and good friend shot her a worried look. Sydney shook it off. Caitlin pulled her in and lifted her chin at Sean. "Mr. Glenn has challenged us to a match. But I know you have the gala tonight to get ready for."

Nick's face fell. "I didn't realize you had something on after this. We thought it would help. We don't want to cause problems."

Sydney laughed. Not a ha-ha funny one but a "what

the hell" one. "Honestly, it's been that kind of day since Chris showed up on my doorstep. It's a nice idea, thank you. What do you say to one set, points to fifteen, two-point spread?"

Sean stuck his hand out to Caitlin. "Deal, Ms. Kelly."

The four of them shook on it and headed to their respective sides of the net. Sydney snagged Caitlin's arm and pulled her over to the boxes she'd stood on earlier. "They wanted to help me out? I think the god of love wanted to help you out. Of your panties," she said, tilting her head toward Sean.

"He may want to, but I'm not that easy. The guy is a man-whore. A stud, but a man-whore. I'll beat him and take his money, but that's it," Caitlin said. Her friend helped her onto the overturned boxes and held her hand to keep her steady while Sydney addressed the crowd.

"Ladies and gentlemen, I thought we were done for the day, but it seems we have a couple of last minute challengers who have proposed a sudden death game to wrap up the Curse the Darkness Beach Volleyball Tournament. The lovely Miss Caitlin Kelly, formerly of Team Veggie Delight, and I will be facing off, mano a mano, with Team Greek, consisting of Nick 'Ares' Thurston and Sean 'Eros' Glenn, for a winner-takes-all-the-glory fifteen-point set." Wow, this public speaking thing is getting easier. Or she was just numb from fear by this point. Sydney continued, "Each side has pledged a thousand dollars for the chance of bragging rights because gambling on the game would be illegal and thus frowned upon since we didn't get a license for that. Hint, hint."

Supportive "boos" floated up from the bleachers.

"Yeah, yeah," Sydney shouted back. "Do we have a

ref?"

The volunteer referee from the game earlier waved from his position on the sidelines.

"All righty then. Players to your positions."

Caitlin helped her off the box, and they shook hands with the actors before ducking under the net to their own side of the court.

The black-haired Caitlin pulled her hair through the loop at the back of her baseball cap. "Um, Syd?"

"Yeah?"

"Did you notice that the crowd's gotten bigger since the tournament ended, not smaller?"

She hadn't until Caitlin had pointed it out. But her friend was right. Most of the tournament and raffle workers were gone, but there were more people on the sidelines than there had been at the earlier game. The few volunteer workers that were left were scrawling receipts as fast as they could write them.

There was more security around the court as well. Sydney motioned for the ref not to start the clock and jogged back to the net. She waved the men over.

"Problem?" Nick asked.

"I'm not sure. Caitlin just pointed out that we have more people now than we did earlier, and then I saw there were more security guys than before. Did you do that or should I be concerned?" she asked.

"No worries. We did that. Sean and I spoke to Martine during your game, and she sent them down just in case."

Sydney frowned. "You knew you were going to be playing?"

"Not until we got here," Sean broke in. "The idea presented itself, and we ran with it. Don't worry, you're in the clear. We have this covered. They were precautionary in case you said yes. We'll be done before the crowds get much bigger. And we took care of transportation home. You and Chris will get the limo back."

"It's all right, Sydney," Nick assured her.

She nodded slowly. "Okay." Then she tossed Sean the ball. "Instead of a coin toss, we've decided to let the challengers serve." Sean's eyes lit up.

As she returned to her partner, Sydney leaned and whispered into Caitlin's ear. "His cousin plays pro. I think he knows what he's doing. Show no mercy." Caitlin bumped her outstretched hand, and they gave the nod to the referee.

The whistle blew, and the carnage started. It was a good thing Caitlin had taken her warning to heart because Sean started with a sneaky serve they barely managed to return. The ball went back and forth a few times before Sydney got in a lucky shot and won the point and control of the ball. Nick was an okay player. Sean was good. Their level of good, maybe better since he was also compensating for his partner.

She'd expected a fun match, but the guys were playing for real. She and Caitlin returned the compliment and went full out. They managed to stay a point ahead until they hit double digits, and then Sean spiked back a serve at the net. Caitlin didn't have time to get out of the way. She managed to twist and take the shot on her upper arm instead of in her face. The force of it knocked her off her feet.

Sean was under the net and crouched by her partner before Sydney had the chance to move. "Oh, shit. Sorry," he said. Nick also beat her to Caitlin, and the men were helping her to her feet by the time Sydney reached her.

"You okay?" Sydney asked.

"I'm fine, I'm fine," Caitlin answered. She looked up at Sean. "Nice spike."

"I am so sorry," the actor apologized again.

Caitlin shrugged their hands off gently. "I'm okay, honestly." She gave them a reassuring wink, then turned to face the crowd. "I've seen better hits come from PBS," she shouted.

Sean hesitated, and she winked at him again. "Nick, I do believe we've been dissed," he replied loudly. "Let's finish this."

"Yeah, Caitlin, let's finish this," Sydney echoed.

The crowd ate it up. The guys scored another point, and then they were leading by one. Sydney set the ball to Caitlin, who was waiting at the corner of the net. She spiked it to a piece of open sand and tied the game at thirteen points each. Sydney prepared to receive her high-five when Caitlin sat in the middle of the court.

"Syd, gotta problem," Caitlin said, her voice flat. She bent one knee and crossed her other ankle over it, holding the arch of her foot with one hand. It took Sydney a minute to see the blood dripping from between Caitlin's fingers.

Sydney snapped her fingers and pointed at the referee. "First aid kit. Now!" She knelt carefully beside Caitlin. "What did you step on?"

Caitlin nudged a piece of brown metal lying on top of the sand. Sydney picked up the rusted beer bottle cap. "When did you get your last tetanus shot?" she asked her friend.

Caitlin groaned. "I'm probably due. I hate those things. They make food taste funny for days."

The referee dropped a plastic case beside them. Sydney pulled out a couple gauze packets and began unwrapping them. She pointed to a roll of medical tape with her elbow. "Will one of you guys get that going for me? I need a couple of four-inch pieces." She brushed the sand off the bottom of Caitlin's foot and gave the oozing wound a swipe with an alcohol wipe. "You're going to need stitches."

"Oh, hurray," Caitlin groaned.

Sean ripped two strips of tape off the roll and handed them to Sydney, who slapped them and the gauze pads onto the sole of Caitlin's foot. "She's done. Call it a draw?"

"Absolutely," Nick agreed. "Rematch next year?"

Sydney felt her face contort in disbelief. Like she'd ever see any of these guys again. "We'll see."

The crowd was surprisingly good with their announcement. As everyone dispersed, the comments coming back to her explained that the reaction was because the game had been fast and furious but mostly because it had been real. Their fans, both of the foundation and the series, appreciated the fact the players played; they hadn't been putting on a show. She and Caitlin and Sean and Nick had fought each other for every point, and everyone knew it.

If they got lucky, the appreciation would have a monetary impact on their bottom line.

Nick and Sean offered to drive Caitlin to a nearby clinic for stitches and shots while Russ called for the car. Security left with them. The tournament volunteer team cleaned up the rest of the site, and the final straggling spectators faded away.

After a final circuit around the court and surrounding area, Sydney dragged herself up the rows of the bleachers and took a seat beside the last remaining onlooker. They sat in silence, staring at the ocean and the late afternoon sun hovering above the horizon.

Sunrise to sunset. That was the deal. Sydney looked at Chris. This was good-bye.

Chapter 19

"Thank you," Chris said. Sydney stared at the shore, tension draining from her shoulders as the waves rolled in and lost their fury as they died on the sand. He stared at her and found the same sense of peace. He hated to break their comfortable silence, but he had fifteen minutes left before sundown, and he didn't want to waste a second of it.

"For what?"

For everything. For the coffee run and Odin and Gary Dobson. For the photo shoot and Robert Clancy and the sunset. "For this," he said simply.

"You're welcome."

She didn't get it.

Chris never had to work at this part. Getting the girl was easy. They played hard to get, but they were plenty easy to catch. Sydney didn't play that game. Maybe it had taken him too long to realize it, but he got it now.

"Was today successful?" he asked.

She laughed. "By whose definition?" He thought he heard a hint of bitter in the response, but then she went on. "Curse the Darkness did great. Much better than I hoped with baskets and stuff. Plus, the volleyball challenge was an extra two thousand out of nowhere. Thank you for that."

"It was only fair. I got exactly what I wanted and then some," Chris told her. "The role was never a sure thing. And I got to spend the day with you."

This time there was no question about the bitter. "You can stop now, Chris."

"Why do you find it so hard to believe?" He looked down at his hands and had to unclench his fists to pull the nails out of his palms. Christ, he knew she was worth it, but she gave stubborn a run for its money.

"In case you missed it in the seventeen million things we did today, there's not a person out there who would consider me Hollywood material."

"I do," Chris argued. "You are not your scars, Sydney. I didn't have the whole picture for most of the day. But now I understand why your grandmother moving the fire extinguisher freaked you out so badly. Why you didn't want to try on a toga." He was sitting right next to her and noticed she'd chosen the side that would put her bad shoulder away from him. He didn't know if she realized what she'd done.

He leaned back and propped his elbows on the bench behind him. Now he could see the scars. They were still bad; she'd never be able to pretend they weren't, but they weren't the worst he'd seen. How could he convince her of that? "Can you tell me about your back? I want to know."

He had her attention. She studied him like an ant under a magnifying glass. It took everything he had not to twitch. She needed to give him a hard look. His words weren't meshing with his earlier actions. Chris was prepared to give her the time she needed.

Sydney closed her eyes and tilted her face into the fading sunlight. "About a year ago there was a car crash."

He waited for more, but nothing else was forthcoming. "Syd, please."

"Okay. Sixteen and a half months ago we—the girls and I—went out to celebrate Vanessa's birthday," she elaborated. "We were having a fun time. Good food. Better ouzo shots. Vanessa and Ashleigh went to the bathroom. Caitlin went to talk to the waiter about bringing out the cake we ordered. I was alone at the table, my back to the window. All of a sudden people were pointing at me, screaming at me. I never had a chance to turn around."

Her eyes were still closed. Chris couldn't tell if she didn't want to look at him as she recounted her story or if she didn't want to risk seeing the scene she was describing if she opened them.

"They say the driver didn't slow down, didn't even tap the brakes before slamming into the building. I was caught in the wreckage when the fire started. Nobody tried to get near me. The flames were too high. The fire department got me out eventually. Weeks in the hospital. Months in therapy. That's where I met most of the guys. I decided that if I survived, I was going to do something with my life. Helping people like me seemed the best way to do that."

"Jesus," he breathed. He wrapped his hand around her nape and squeezed gently.

Sydney pulled away and stared straight out onto the beach. "And that's my tragic tale."

Chris stared into the sun with her. That was…so much worse than anything he'd imagined. Then a thought that made him shiver crossed his mind. "Was Layla at the restaurant? Was she one of the people who didn't help you? Is that how you know her?"

That got her to meet his gaze. "Chris, Layla was the driver."

He was almost on his feet before she yanked him back down. "Fucking bitch! What else did she do to you?" he demanded.

"That was enough, don't you think?"

"Tell me."

"I can't."

"Sydney!" And he'd thrown the two of them together twice this afternoon. God!

"I can't. Legally. I can't say anything else. It was part of the settlement that paid my medical bills."

"I hate her," Chris spat.

Sydney elbowed him gently in the ribs. "Me, too. Although I did win twenty bucks because of her this afternoon. Pay up."

Chris was sitting on the bleachers with a beautiful woman. His blood pressure was rising and breath was coming faster, and it was all for the wrong reasons.

She nudged him again. "It's done. I'm here. Let it go. You can't let it poison you. Trust me, I know."

Sydney obviously didn't want to discuss it anymore. She was giving him the same look he'd seen others give her that afternoon on the volleyball court. Sympathy. He wasn't the one she should be feeling sorry for, but she obviously wasn't going to feel it for herself. He might be feeling pissed off, but this wasn't about him. He had to remember that. If she wanted to change the subject, he was more than willing. "So, can I?"

"Can you what?" she asked.

"See you tonight? Will you save me a dance at your gala?" he pressed.

The sunset was beautiful, but the dimming light was throwing shadows in all the wrong places. He couldn't see if it was the light or if she was blushing. A blush would be a good sign. A blush would be fantastic.

"Probably."

There was a smile. A small one, but it was genuine. "Can you save me all of them?"

"That depends," she teased.

He was about to ask what his fate rode on when his phone interrupted. He recognized the ring. His agent was calling. It had to be news from High Note. He'd been specific that nothing else was important enough to interrupt the afternoon. Chris grabbed the bench with both hands and tried to relax. If he wanted Sydney to believe he could make her come first, it started now.

"Who is it?"

"No one important. Depends on what?"

"Chris." She put a world of exasperation into one word. "Who is it?"

"My agent. It can wait."

"It's about the movie, isn't it?"

She wasn't going to let it go. "Yes. Probably."

"Answer it."

"It can wait." At least until the end of this conversation. Thankfully, the phone fell silent.

Sydney leaned back until her shoulders rested against the bench he was stretched out on. She tilted her head and tapped it on his shoulder. "Business calls happen. You can call them back." God, she felt good against him.

"Nope. We need to settle this first. What will it take to get all of your dances?"

"Your checkbook. I'm one of the bachelorettes on the auction block tonight. One dance only."

"Okay, so I can buy all of your dances tonight," Chris confirmed.

His phone rang again. Different ring. He had to check that one. He frowned at the call display. Answering was unavoidable, but the call was short. Sydney's car was waiting on the street.

"Sunrise to sunset," he said as an explanation.

She nodded. Chris took her hand and helped her down the bleachers. She didn't need the help; her balance was fine. He wasn't about to pass up on a perfect excuse though. Lights flashed to the side of them. He didn't look. He didn't want to know if it was Benny with a final shot or somebody else with less noble intentions. Let them take pictures. If he had his way there would be a lot more of him and Sydney.

Two town cars idled in the no parking zone where the beach walk met the road. Sydney had scooted to the far side of the vehicle and fastened her seatbelt when his phone went off again.

"Save those dances for me. I'll see you tonight," Chris said.

"Answer your phone."

He went to his knee on the car seat and leaned across to where Sydney was seated behind the driver. He was so going to steal a kiss. Karma gave him this opportunity; it would be wasteful and ungrateful not to take advantage.

It turned out he didn't have to steal it. Sydney gave it to him. Unlike their first kiss, this time she touched him. Her fingertips touched his temple and then trailed down his jaw. When she got to his lips, she pulled away and looked at him through shining eyes. He grabbed her shoulder and tugged her forward again. She tasted like sunshine and chocolate icing.

Sometime during the kiss, his phone had stopped ringing and had started again. "I'll see you tonight," he repeated. "I promise."

"Good-bye, Chris," she whispered.

"See you later," he corrected.

He crawled out of the car, shut the door, and let her go. This was not good-bye. He wouldn't let it be. He ducked into his own car and instructed the driver to stop at the studio before taking him home. He needed to pick something up.

His agent couldn't decide on ecstatic or furious. Ecstatic because Chris had evidently impressed Robert Clancy enough to be offered the job. Furious because said Mr. Clancy wanted to meet him for drinks to discuss it further and Chris wasn't picking up the phone.

Honest to God, he should have worn a cup today. Karma was giving him the workout of his life. This was a replay of this afternoon with the added benefit of knowing how the play was going to turn out. Get the part or get the girl? What was really funny was he wanted the girl to read the part before he said yes.

He'd been working this idea since he'd spoken to Gary Dobson. That industry genius ran projects past his non-industry wife, and she knew what she liked from an audience point-of-view. Sydney had great, compatible taste in classic movies. And current television, not to put too fine a point on things. She loved entertainment, not the entertainment business. He was interested in what she thought of the project.

After much badgering, Chris got Clancy's phone number and made the call himself. He hoped it was the right call.

"Hi, Robert, it's Chris Peck. How are you tonight?"

The producer's deep bass sounded happy to hear from him. "Fine, Chris. How was your day as a slave?"

"It was fine. Martine Peeples said it was a huge hit on the social media sites. Apparently other media outlets are starting to pick up on it."

"Good to hear. Would you be free for drinks this evening to start discussions?"

"Actually, I have Valentine's plans with Sydney tonight," Chris said. He didn't choke on the words. Maybe that was a sign he'd done the right thing.

"Oh, her fundraising gala is tonight. Your agent said. Of course you'd want to finish off the charity's evening. That's good planning. You can't buy positive publicity like that."

Chris' chin hit his chest. So easy. It would be so easy

to agree with him, to say that he was doing it for his career. It would cover his ass and impress High Note's backers. Press was everything when it came to launching a movie.

But it would be a lie. Another of his mother's sayings came back to him. Start as you mean to continue. He didn't mean to start like that, but he had; now he wanted to finish it. He might not have known how this conversation was going to go, but he was not being impulsive. Pros and cons were noted. He didn't try to figure out the karmic feedback either. The right thing was the right thing.

"The studio doesn't know. I'm doing this as me, not as Zeus. There won't be any press."

A surprising voice of censure came over the line. "That's not very practical. Like you said earlier, you were prepared to do what it took to make the sweepstakes work for you, but now that the contest is over you can walk away and quit wasting your time."

Chris flinched when his words from his conversation with Clancy that afternoon were thrown back at him. "The contest is over, but it's not a waste of my time," Chris protested. "I asked Sydney if I could see her later, and she agreed."

"That's a risky game. If the tabloids find out you're only dating her until the contract is signed…"

Chris' gut clenched. He must have done a better job of dismissing Sydney this afternoon than he originally thought. "I'm going out with her because I like her. And thankfully she's the forgiving sort because I didn't make a great first impression with her."

A long silence. Long enough that Chris checked to see if they'd been disconnected. "I understand," Clancy finally said.

"I hope you do. I told you I agreed to be the sweepstakes prize precisely for this chance. I want the role. Badly. But…"

"But you want the girl too. And if you had to pick?"

Silence weighed on them both.

"You surprised me, Chris. Now I owe Gary dinner," the producer said.

"Gary?"

"Gary Dobson. We were chatting this afternoon about you."

"You talked to Gary Dobson today? About me?" About mouthing off about "his Sydney". God, shoot me now.

"I've known Gary for years. I told him you were all business, but he was certain you'd choose Sydney in the end. Did he tell you he got me my start? Not that I'll admit where. That job won't be listed in IMDb. But he was right again. I really should stop betting against him. He has a secret weapon."

"Arlene," Chris blurted out.

Clancy laughed. "You do know them."

"We met. Please say hi for me the next time you see them."

"Okay. I'll let you know where I ended up taking them for dinner."

Robert would let him know? Why would he be in contact again? "Robert, to be clear, when you said that I chose Sydney, you meant over the part, didn't you?"

"Drinks, Chris. Over drinks. I'm not fool enough to decide on an actor, have my opinion validated by Gary Dobson, and then change my mind when he wants to go out with a pretty girl on Valentine's Day. I'll call you on Monday. Enjoy your weekend."

"You too, Robert," Chris barely got out before the

call ended.

He threw himself back into the seat, utterly exhausted. He'd had his fair share of auditions. That, by far, topped the list.

Chapter 20

Sydney frowned at the mirror. She'd hoped to be able to recreate the look the stylists had given her that afternoon, but between the makeup and the hair she was falling short. She'd paid enough attention to remember a couple of the tricks they'd used. An afternoon in the sun hadn't helped her freckles though. She gave her half-upswept hair another shot of hairspray and forced a smile. There was nothing in her teeth; she was good to go.

Ashleigh was waiting in her living room. The Scandinavian blonde looked stunning in a floor-length gown that was two shades darker blue than her eyes. She wore deceptively short heels that gave the illusion of being much higher than they were. Sydney wasn't a clotheshorse, but she knew two things: the dress would be from a consignment shop, and the heels would be the real thing. Dancers didn't skimp on shoes.

Caitlin was waiting there as well. The dark Hispanic-Irish actress tugged up her cream-colored wrap from where it had slid and gathered at her elbow. The bruise on her biceps where the volleyball hit her was starting to bloom. Sydney saw that the padded bandage on her foot stretched the straps of her friend's sandals, but she only noticed because she knew where to look. Caitlin had smiled gamely when asked if she was up for this evening but admitted she'd only be having one dance with her bad foot.

They met her with wolf-whistles. Sydney's dress was a shot silk, green in one light, gray in another. She'd originally bought the strapless gown because it came with a little bolero type jacket. Tonight she'd left the jacket in the closet. It was time for her to step into the spotlight.

It was a shame the limo service hadn't lasted into the

evening. The trio piled into Ashleigh's ancient compact and toodled along in no danger of breaking speed limits in the sometimes functioning car. Ashleigh parked it herself in the back lot of the Pacific Western Hotel where they'd booked the smallest, cheapest ballroom they could get for the foundation's gala.

It wasn't a Hollywood gala in some swanky club. It was a chain hotel not too far from the airport. The tables had white tablecloths and centerpieces put together by the gala's setup committee, some of whom were in the car with her. That's what Vanessa and Ashleigh had been doing all morning before the tournament. The decorations were balloons and streamers, and there'd been a hell of a battle about there being a cash bar or not. They'd tried to be frugal without crossing the line into cheap. Sydney hadn't seen the final result, but she was hopeful.

She let the pair in the front seats chatter as she focused on her breathing. Curse the Darkness was her baby. Her family had helped out as best they could from a distance, and her friends had been insanely generous with their time, but she didn't think they truly understood how big this was. This was the charity's first year. But Sydney wanted big. Years of working the complaints switchboard of the hospital's billing center followed by a year of recovery had given her perspective, both on how huge the need for help was and how to make it work. She knew the system from the inside out. And knowing how to use it meant knowing how to work it. She wanted to make sure everyone got as much out of their treatment as she did.

It was funny. She'd never minded meeting new people. It was the attention from the public speaking and the photos that freaked her out. She had never liked having her picture taken before the accident. Now it was a million times worse. This afternoon's mind mush at being thrust into a gaggle of movie stars notwithstanding, she generally did pretty well in groups. Spending the day with Chris had forced her to face facts. If she wanted to make this a national charity, she'd have to step up. Today had proven she could do it. With the money they'd already raised, including the huge, unexpected bump from the publicity Olympus had generated, Sydney had a shot at taking this to the next level. Having had some experience with once in a lifetime opportunities, she was going to grab on to this one and run, for herself and everyone after her.

It was ironic that the guy who had started out the day helping himself had ended up being the reason she'd be able to help herself and so many others.

Despite his promise, and Sydney felt he truly believed he meant it this time, she didn't really expect any Greek gods to dance attendance on her tonight. Once Chris had undone his cranial-rectal inversion, he had turned out to be a pretty nice guy. Good kisser. Excellent kisser. Sydney drifted for a moment as she'd played back their three kisses. She may not have ended up with the guy, but he'd definitely given her enough memories to stop hating Valentine's Day.

God, they were there. Sydney caught herself reaching for her shoulder and forced her hand back to her side. The girls stopped at the fire doors that led to the corridor that led to the ballroom. From here on out, she wasn't the same Sydney Chris had seen all afternoon. Now she was the star.

She pasted on a smile when they walked down the hall. By the time they hit the ballroom it was genuine. The room looked amazing. It didn't look like a little fundraiser at all. It looked like a gala. They hadn't been close to selling out of tickets, but the room looked fuller than it should have. It might have been all the decorations. She didn't want to know where some of the more elaborate displays came from, and she certainly wasn't going to ask. They'd be gone by morning, and if all the meetings with lawyers had taught her anything in the last year, plausible deniability was her friend. Besides, there was so much more to see.

These were her people. A familiar face greeted her from every group, and if one didn't, she made sure she went to introduce herself. Sydney was halfway around the room when she dropped into a covered chair at a half-empty table. "Hi, Nana. Hi, Mrs. D."

Her grandmother didn't fit in among the small business people and the everyday middle-class crowd. Of course, Sydney hadn't expected Marilyn Monroe to try. Mrs. Dobson surprised her by decking herself out as if she were at an after-party for an awards show. She complimented both women on looking so glamorous. That was when Mr. Dobson came up behind her and offered her a glass of wine. He'd gone full out as well, his gray hair complimenting his silver bowtie and cummerbund of his tuxedo. "Did I miss a memo?" Sydney asked. "I'm pretty sure we decided on formal not black tie."

"I couldn't let the ladies show me up," he explained. Then he stopped.

"And?" Sydney prompted.

"I wouldn't want to ruin the surprise."

Sydney groaned, "Do you have any idea how many surprises I've had today? I'm set for a decade at least."

Mrs. Dobson laughed. "I think you'll be good for one more."

"Nana, help me out here, would you please?" Sydney pleaded.

"I would, but they won't tell me what's going on. Where is your date?"

"I'm working tonight, Nana."

"That hunk of a god isn't here yet?"

"No, he's not coming. The sweepstakes prize ended this afternoon."

"I've known actors," the old lady said, with an emphasis on the "known" that Sydney could have gone lifetimes without hearing, "and Zeus was looking at you like you were the last spoonful of ambrosia. He'll be back."

"Okay, Nana. I've got to keep circulating."

"Before you go…" She pulled Sydney down and whispered in her ear. "I left the extinguisher under the sink today."

Sydney patted the old woman's hand. "That's great. Thank you," she whispered back.

She finished her second circuit before she admitted it was working. Tickets for silent auction baskets were going. Vanessa and Trent were making regular runs to the bank's night deposit. People smiled and drank and mingled and seemed to be having a good time.

Obviously it had to end. The lights in the ballroom went up, and there was no place to hide. Ashleigh caught her eye, and Caitlin took over the microphone at the podium in the corner for her introduction. Unlike the volleyball speeches, this one had been prepared for weeks. She'd had it memorized for almost as long. It didn't stop her from pulling her cue cards from her purse though.

Caitlin finished with her introduction, and Sydney joined her at the microphone, not flinching once at the cameras that were going off in front of her. It seemed like a lot of cameras, but she had nothing to compare it to.

Most looked to be held by friends, and she assumed the rest were people writing off their tickets as a charitable expense.

The welcome went well. Thanking the sponsors went off without a hitch. The raffle draw was thankfully handled by a friend from work so she got to take a breather for twenty minutes. And then Sydney was back for the night's big event. The bachelor/bachelorette auction. They had an even dozen volunteers who had written their own biographies, including Ashleigh, who presented her newly opened Jessup Dance Studios as being owned by the honorary granddaughter of Fred Astaire and Ginger Rogers' fictional love child, and Caitlin, who'd billed herself as a movie starlet on hiatus from the paparazzi after such diverse roles as Victim Number Two in an alphabet-titled crime drama episode of the week and the pretzel-offering stewardess in a comedy that only lasted a week in the theaters. Sydney's fellow patients had even rounded up four men and one woman in dress uniform.

She was stunned. She wasn't a professional auctioneer, but the bids were insane. The second bachelor sold for almost three thousand dollars. Caitlin told her to hold steady and keep going. So she did. She almost fainted at the numbers, but the checks kept being written and the bids kept coming. She scratched the eleventh name off her list and looked at the last. Number twelve. Sydney Richardson. She pulled out her bio.

And suddenly she wasn't at the microphone anymore. Gary Dobson stepped into her place as if he'd planned it, and she found herself front and center in the spotlight with Vanessa and Caitlin blocking her exits. "Traitors!"

The man did have presence; Gary Dobson was a man

people listened to. In front of a crowd he was electrifying. As the target of his attention, he was somewhat terrifying.

She didn't mind the round of applause for the bachelors and bachelorettes who had gone before her, nor the thanks to the bidders, although those were supposed to be her lines. But he was gearing up to something, and everyone seemed to know what it was but her.

"Miss Sydney Richardson is the reason we've all gathered here tonight. She imagined Curse the Darkness, plotted and planned it, and invited us here to bring it to life. I don't know how much we've raised, but I hope we've exceeded her expectations. Now we have one more chance to do that. Our last bachelorette tonight has a reserve bid of five thousand dollars."

Sydney whipped around. "I have what? Who? When did this happen? Is it even allowed?"

"Apparently she neglected to list 'reporter' on her resume with all of those questions," the man continued.

"Six thousand dollars," a man's voice called from the back of the crowd over the laughter.

"Sixty-five hundred," Gary Dobson said into the microphone.

"Seven thousand," the voice called again.

"Seven thousand?" she croaked. She'd doubled the best bid of the night. And she still couldn't see who was bidding.

"Eight thousand." The voice was closer now and clearer since the surrounding din had died off. She was pretty sure she recognized the tuxedo.

"Son, you do realize you're bidding against yourself, don't you?" the auctioneer said.

"Ten thousand, and that's my final offer."

Sydney skipped back a couple steps and reached over the podium, twisting the microphone until it faced her. "Sold!" she screeched.

It was the last thing she said for a while. The crowd parted, and Chris appeared once again in his tux. He'd looked fine in the bright morning light, but tuxedos were made for the night. Sydney heard the auction wrapping up behind her and Mr. Dobson thanking everyone, but at that moment she didn't care. He was there. He stopped in front of her and smiled. The lights dimmed, but she didn't move.

She blinked a couple times when his lips moved and no sound came out. "Hi," she greeted him.

"Hi." His smile got bigger as he looked at her. That was nice. "You look amazing," he said.

"So do you." It wasn't fair. This morning she'd met him pre-caffeine and wearing pajamas, and she'd been perfectly fine with his sparkling hazel eyes and brushed back brown hair. Tonight she was dressed to the nines and awake and was about to swallow her own tongue.

"Yeah, I'm all Double-Oh-Seven," he agreed.

"Connery or Moore?"

"Now I feel better." Chris held out his hand to her. He pulled her in and started to sway. Sydney trailed her hands up his biceps and twined them around his neck. He pulled her in a little closer. "Sorry I'm late. Did I miss any dances?"

"Nope. This is my first." Hey, the power of conversation had returned.

"Excellent." He twirled her around, and she spun with him. Years of being Ashleigh's practice dance partner and class fill-in paid off in one move.

Cue the John Hughes sigh as Molly Ringwald got the guy. It was practically perfect. Except…

"I seem to recall you saying I'd get a kiss at the end

of the day, no tongue, if I asked nicely," Sydney said.

"I did say that," Chris agreed.

The music had stopped, but they were still moving. Maybe it had just stopped for everyone else. "I also recall saying I wouldn't be the one asking," she continued.

"You're going to make me ask again?"

Sydney smiled. "You actually haven't asked yet."

Chris' hand slipped up her back. Right over her scar, and his face didn't even flicker. "I think I remember that. You know what I like best about your gala tonight and this dance in particular?"

"What's that?"

His smile was full of all kinds of ideas. "I didn't have to sign a terms of service agreement."

The End

Publisher's Note

Please help this author's career by posting an honest review wherever you purchased this book.

About Elle Rush

Elle Rush is a Canadian romance author from Winnipeg, Manitoba. When she's not travelling, she's hard at work writing her contemporary romance eBooks which are set all over the world. Elle earned a degree in Spanish and French, barely passed German, and is starting to learn Italian and Filipino. She has flunked poetry in every language she's ever taken. She also has mild addictions to tea, cookbooks and the sci-fi channel. Keep up with her new releases by subscribing to her newsletter at www.ellerush.com/newsletter.

Made in the USA
Middletown, DE
18 March 2017